THE BELLWETHER
RULES FOR THE DEAD

I0592800

KERRY MITCHELL

A Birdy Black Book

Birdy Black Books
Melbourne

Book Layout © 2017 BookDesignTemplates.com
Printed by Ingram Spark USA

The Bellwether Rules for the Dead/ Kerry Mitchell. -- 1st ed.
ISBN 978-0-6482301-2-0

{For the dearly departed}

As KEEPER OF THE BELLWETHER FAMILY CRYPT, I HAVE SWORN TO TAKE THEIR SECRETS TO THE GRAVE. BUT SINCE I'M DEAD, I SUPPOSE IT WOULD DO NO HARM TO SPILL A RULE OR TWO...

THE RULES

$\{ 8\!\!-\!\!\pi \}$

Woe, destruction, ruin and decay;
The worst is death,
And death will have his day.

Act III, Scene 2 - Richard II
William Shakespeare

Dead bodies demand immediate attention

They used to say that not even a ghost would wish to haunt the halls of the Bellwether house but that was before Great Aunt Prunella passed away. It happened a very long time ago and I'm a little fuzzy on the details but I think that was when Mildread and Maudelin (still dressed in their funeral attire) moved into the big old house on the hill, along with their father, Byron Bellwether.

The house was gloomy and grim, but then so were the Bellwethers, so I would say it was a perfect fit.

It sat precariously perched on the edge of a crumbling clifftop and from Mildread and Maudelin's bedroom window you could see the crashing waves below, so naturally they felt right at home.

Sometimes in the middle of the night, they would press their noses up against the chilly windowpane, scaring anyone passing by almost witless for they would see two glum girls, one a mirror image to the other, staring down upon them; the candle on their windowsill the only light guiding them through Wildend.

That's what they called the stretch of land that ran high above the sea at the tip of Bitterly Bay.

The broken lighthouse, looming silently in the dark, provided no hope to the lost mariner so they would gather up what little courage remained and steer their vessel away from what they believed was a ghostly image reflected double in the windowpane of a spectre portending their untimely death.

If they made it out of that treacherous cove still alive and kicking, they would thank their lucky stars above instead of Mildread and Maudelin. Some would even go so far as to curse them, such is the plight of the misunderstood.

Mildread and Maudelin were not inclined to dwell on the many failings of man and so they continued to sit at their window and stare out to sea (and silently save the lost souls sailing by).

Behind the house was a wild wood that had never properly been explored and so no name had properly been given to it. It was just known as Wildwood.

It was so thick and impenetrable that it was widely believed (as most things were in Bitterly Bay) that no one had ever gone in there or ever come out.

But they were wrong, of course.

On the grounds of the Bellwether estate, between the dark and sinister Wildwood and the slightly forlorn and decaying house, was the graveyard where Mildread and Maudelin liked to spend a miserable afternoon.

On this particular day, Maudelin was sitting on a mound of dirt that belonged to Aunt Prunella. On such a perfect day (and by that I mean ominous and bleak) she liked to sit outside in the crackling air and watch the storm brew.

She was reading a book with a hairy, black spider that had crawled across the page. Her long black hair trailed the words like fingers on braille. Six angry hornets, heading back to the hollow in the dead tree behind the wild hedgerow, took a quick look over her shoulder, not disturbing her in the least, but the story was obviously not interesting enough to make them stay and so they buzzed away.

Usually the animals and insects were avid readers of Maudelin's books. If she accidentally left one in the garden overnight, the snails would devour every page. And don't get me started on the worms, or the book-worms as I call them.

Mildread, never far from Maudelin, was picking blackberries for Olga to put in a pie. She liked the way the thorns grabbed at her hair and skin and clothing, as if trying to gobble her up, and she liked the way the berries stained her fingers black. If you ask me, she had magic in those fingertips. They both did. It was widely believed they held hands in their mother's womb and, ever since, there'd been a little bit of magic in the air whenever they touched. Objects moved about of their own accord. And being twins, one always seemed to know what the other was thinking.

For example, Mildread had stopped picking berries and was staring at the ground when Maudelin said, 'Crows?' which wouldn't make sense to anyone for you look up when you spy a bird and not down. It just so happens, though, that Mildread was staring at an object in the soil beneath the blackberry bush and thinking, *the crows have been collecting bones again.*

Crows can predict rain. A murder of crows (for that is what a group of them are called) would gather at the edge of Wildwood whenever a storm approached, which can be a little disconcerting (unless you're Mildread or Maudelin). Sometimes they carried sticks in their beaks, or carrion (dead putrefying flesh), sometimes bones. So when Mildread spotted a bone poking out of the earth, she naturally assumed that a crow had found the thorny blackberry bush as inviting as she had.

Mildread pulled at the muddy bone. 'It's stuck. I think it's attached to something.'

Maudelin wrenched her eyes away from her book, placed a black feather in the margin to mark her spot, and said, 'Attached to what?'

Mildread pulled harder and out popped…

'A hand, do you think it belongs to Aunt Prunella?'

'No,' said Maudelin, patting the undisturbed earth beneath her feet and leaning against the gravestone, 'she's right where we left her.'

Mildread took a closer look under the blackberry bush.

'It's not just a hand,' she said, poking about in the dirt with a stick. 'There's a clavicle and skull… and a complete corpse, if I'm not mistaken.'

She knew a lot about dead bodies because the Bellwethers were undertakers and rule number one dictates that dead bodies demand immediate attention. You don't have to be a mind reader to know that Mildread and Maudelin were thinking the same thing at the exact same moment. And so Mildread collected her rusty tin bucket of berries and untangled her hair from the thorns, and Maudelin took a last, longing look at the overcast sky, then, watched by a murder of crows lining up along the hedgerow, they walked down the overgrown path to their back door.

The book and the spider stayed behind.

Never make fun of the dead

W hen they reached the kitchen, they said in unison, 'Olga, call the police.'

Olga, the Russian cook, was making the pastry for her blackberry pie. She looked up from her work and said, 'Why?'

'There's a rotting corpse in the blackberry bush.'

'I see.'

Olga lifted the heavy black receiver to her ear and a nasally voice said, 'Number please.' When Olga said, 'The police,' she was put through immediately to an officer who said, 'What is your emergency?'

'A dead body,' said Olga.

'Right you are,' said the officer and two constables were promptly dispatched to the Bellwether house.

'What have we here?' said Constable Ray.

'A body you say?' said Constable Jay.

'Yes,' said Mildread. 'It's buried under the blackberry bush.'

'How did it get there?'

'I haven't the faintest clue but I'm pretty sure it didn't crawl there on its own.'

'So it's definitely deceased then?'

'See for yourself.'

Mildread pointed out the window and beneath the bush the bony hand poked out of the soil.

Maudelin, never far from Mildread, was staring at the hand with an expression that was neither horrified nor frightened. In fact, if such a thing were possible when staring at a decomposing limb, I would say she almost looked a little disappointed.

It's to be expected, I suppose. When you think about it, the excitement over a dead body is all in the discovery. After that they don't do much at all.

And whilst there is nothing unusual about a corpse in a graveyard, you must keep in mind that all of the bodies were properly buried in wooden coffins with lids nailed firmly shut and every tomb had a stone above it to tell you who it was that lay buried six feet under.

Some of the dead had tombstones that were cracked in two or sinking under choking vines, some of the names were hard to read, some of the earth sank deeper in places where it shouldn't, but all of the dearly departed were properly buried.

None had been thrown into a shallow grave under the blackberry bush. And yet that bony hand said otherwise.

'Your father hasn't had any bodies wandering off from the morgue, has he?' chuckled Constable Ray.

Mildread gave him a deathly stare, no doubt recalling rule number two: never make fun of the dead. Poor Maudelin was perilously close to becoming completely disinterested when out of the corner of her eye she caught sight of a tiny movement from deep within the unexplored wood at the end of the garden next door.

A thrilling uneasy feeling stirred deep within her bones.

And because of their uncanny closeness, Mildread felt it too.

Someone was watching them from deep within Wildwood. Could it have anything to do with the body in the blackberry bush? The back of Maudelin's neck prickled. In your case (and mine, too) this would be an unwelcome event but Maudelin perked right up.

Mildread nodded. 'I feel it, too. Someone is in there.'

They weren't exactly giddy with glee but that uneasy feeling settled once again in their bones and they leant eagerly into it.

Once the corpse had been removed and the police had finally left (after enjoying a slice of blackberry pie),

Mildread and Maudelin went back outside to examine the blackberry patch.

There was a gaping hole right in the middle of the bush. It had fought back valiantly and had managed to ensnare a constable or two and extract quite a bit of blood in the process but eventually it had given up its spoils.

'Luckily nothing can kill a blackberry bush,' said Mildread. 'It'll be thick and thorny in no time.'

Maudelin was not so philosophical. Whoever had dug out the dead body had given no consideration to her abandoned book. It now lay half-buried in the dirt, its pages torn, its cover cracked, and a dirty great boot-print splattered across the page where Jane Eyre had once said that she was no bird and no net ensnared her. Maudelin could have become quite bitter about this but Jane's delightfully doomed chum, Helen Burns, said life was too short to be spent in nursing animosity or registering wrongs and so Maudelin decided that if one was going to read such a fine book as *Jane Eyre* (full of delicious bleakness) then one ought to adopt the ideas portrayed within, especially since Jane was such a sensible, forthright girl.

As if one, Mildread and Maudelin turned away from the ruined earth and allowed their gaze once more to fall on the dark Wildwood.

Alive is better than dead

If you were a bird and able to fly high above Bitterly Bay you would see that a lot of trees were crowded into Wildwood. It took up a lot of space on the island of Bitterly Bay. But clearly it would not be the only thing that you would see.

The town, nestled in the bay, had tall, narrow cottages with grey terracotta roofs squashed together in a tight bundle that crept along the cove. They used to crawl up the hill, like black marks on a treasure map leading to the place where X marks the spot – in this case the broken lighthouse – but all the houses along the clifftop had crumbled into the sea until all that remained was the lighthouse and the Bellwether house, clinging to the edge of the cliff.

And squished in between the two was a crooked little cottage that looked abandoned and really ought to have been but somehow wasn't. It was so hidden away behind trees that most people forgot it was even there. This was Crow Cottage. Crows were usually solitary creatures but not these ones. They sat on the roof and scratched at the windowpanes and circled the chimney pot.

They cawed into the darkness in the middle of the night.

But they were not the only occupants of Crow Cottage for Birdy Black lived here with a most unusual girl named Jet. The story goes that Birdy found Jet one dark and stormy night on the doorstep when she was just a baby, wrapped up tight against the weather with eyes wide open to the world. Strange that no one ever stopped to ponder why a baby would be left at the door of such a dilapidated cottage when directly next door there stood the grand Bellwether manse.

Perhaps its gloominess had put them off.

Despite this, Jet rather liked living beneath a lighthouse. It didn't really matter to her that it was broken because she quite liked the idea of a lighthouse refusing to do what everyone expected of it. Jet never did what was expected of her. She was a bit like a lighthouse, if truth be told: bursting forth and blinding all in her brilliance.

She wore her hair in a messy topknot with lots of tendrils hanging down. It looked like a bird's nest on her head. (Don't tell her I said that.) Her clothes were always dishevelled and full of holes and tears where a branch had snagged at them or some wild animal's claws had scratched at them. It always looked like she dressed in a hurry in the dark, which was probably true. Her shoes were always scuffed and Jet didn't even have time to tie her shoelaces.

She was also insatiably curious about everything. You would think that one as curious and fearless as she would have already explored every inch of that dark and spooky wood. But she had not. For Birdy had warned her many times that Wildwood was full of sinister foreboding and malicious intent.

Naturally this made her want to go in there.

But Birdy had said, 'No. Promise me you will never go in there.'

Jet promised. She even crossed her heart and spat on the mat. So that was that.

And because Jet could not go in, Mildread and Maudelin felt it was only fair that they steered clear of Wildwood, too. Besides, maybe Birdy was right. Maybe there were sinister, malicious creatures lurking within, just waiting to devour them. Rule number three: alive is better than dead. (That's not actually a rule but I think it should be.)

And that's not to say they didn't get as close to Wildwood as they could. There was an old wooden stile at the end of the garden behind Crow Cottage – just a few planks of splintered, rotting wood, poking its way between a tiny gap in the thicket and thorn – but beggars can't be choosers. Beside it stood a plum tree, ancient and gnarled, and sometimes the girls would climb it and shimmy across the mossy, thick branch that stretched itself over the hedgerow so that they could sit amongst the shadows of the trees. Sometimes they'd dangle a leg into the gloom and let a blood-plum drop or a dead leaf flutter fitfully down to the ground.

But that was all they ever did.

There had never been a reason to do any more than that.

But now a body had been discovered beneath the blackberry bush and Maudelin was convinced that someone was watching them from Wildwood and Mildread thought that something ought to be done about it, so they left the book buried under the dirt and the blackberries in utter disarray and together they climbed over the low stone wall into Jet's garden.

As usual, though, Jet was one step ahead of them.

She was crouching down behind the wild hedgerow and peering through the narrow gap at the stile. When the twins finally joined her, Jet quickly pulled them down into her hiding crouch.

'There's something moving in Wildwood,' she whispered.

'We know,' said Mildread.

'Don't breathe or it will hear you and then it's all over for us. Are you breathing?'

'No.'

'Me neither,' breathed Maudelin.

'What…did…you…see?' Mildread was trying not to breathe.

Jet shook her head and refused to say another word. She slowly stood up, every movement careful and measured, until she was level with the splintered steps. They were covered in lichen and moss, which made them slippery and slimy, so Jet rubbed her heel across the wood to roughen it up so that she could step carefully onto the stile and swat at a blood-plum hanging precariously on the overhanging branch. It dropped into Wildwood.

'See that?' she said.

'See what?' said Mildread (who was looking in one direction), and Maudelin (who was looking in the other).

'The plum. Did you see the way it fell?'

'What do you mean?'

'I mean it didn't fall straight from the tree,' said Jet. 'It hung in mid-air for just a split-second. And the air all around it went shimmery and shaky. And that means there's some form of magic hovering in Wildwood. And you know what makes magic, don't you?'

'What?'

'Witches,' breathed Jet.

'What are witches doing in the woods?'

'Exactly,' said Jet. 'That's just my point.'

Let the dead lie

Now I don't know if you're the type that believes in witches and the like, but I feel you should know that Jet was a little obsessed with the creatures. She had what is known as a fertile imagination. When Jet first heard this she mistakenly thought Birdy had said 'furtive' instead of 'fertile'. Furtive is a rather secretive and urgent trait. Fertile just means that she had a vivid imagination.

Jet preferred to think of herself as having a furtive imagination.

She loved all things dark and creepy and had a morbid fascination for dead things, like empty bug shells and dried up skeletons of little birds and insects so, as you can imagine, when she first laid eyes upon the rather bleak-looking Bellwether twins, it was compatibility at first sight.

Sometimes friendships can be formed in an instant. Have you ever noticed that? You take one look at someone and you just know, deep in your gut, that you are going to like this person. And that they are going to like you back. And then you can trust them with your deepest, darkest secrets.

(I like to think that you and I share this bond. I felt a tingle down my spine the instant you opened this book. We are connected now, you and I.)

And so it was for Mildread and Maudelin. They had yet to meet a witch and, therefore, could not say one way or the other if they were real or not, but just because you have not seen something that doesn't mean it doesn't exist. There are plenty of things in this world that we cannot see; ghosts, for example. Not everyone can see those. But if you were paying close attention at the beginning of my tale, you will know that I am a ghost. They call me The Ghost of the River Grim because that is where I drowned, deep within the dark wood. Whilst I am sure that you cannot see me, there can be no doubt that you hear my voice forming these words in your head.

Think about that, why don't you.

Mildread and Maudelin also believed in ghosts but that's probably because they lived with one.

As I have already explained, they came to live in the Bellwether house after Aunt Prunella passed away and she was, as the story goes, now a ghost. Her body was buried in the family graveyard but her spirit remained, sight unseen, in the attic. She continued to clean the house (thus 'haunting' every crack and crevice of this crumbling edifice) because in her opinion certain standards must not be allowed to slip simply because one is dead. One must never let death get in the way of a cobweb.

Few people outside of the house, though, were inclined to acknowledge her existence but Jet positively adored her. She saw little difference between a witch and a ghost. If you believed in one, then you must surely believe in the other, therefore she was willing to believe that witches were lurking in the woods.

Mildread knew that what she was about to say next would thrill Jet to the core.

'We found a body in the blackberry bush.'

It's all very well to talk of witches lurking in Wildwood but without actual proof it's just wishes in the wind. Jet was convinced that witches were definitely the sort that would bury a body but that still didn't explain why they would choose to bury it beneath the blackberry bush. Why not stay hidden deep in Wildwood and bury the body out there?

'First things first,' she said, not willing to jump to any conclusions. 'Show me the spot where the body was found.'

And so they returned to the scene of the crime, so to speak.

'Are you sure it's not Aunt P?' asked Jet.

'How does she get from there,' said Mildread, pointing to Prunella's gravestone, 'over to there?'

'Maybe she's a zombie and crawled there on her own.'

'Doubt it,' said Maudelin. 'Zombies are flesh-eaters. They don't generally crawl from one gravesite to another. And, besides, Aunt Prunella is not a zombie. She's a ghost.'

(I, for one, am very glad they make this distinction.)

'We ought to dig her up,' said Jet, 'and make sure her bones are where they're supposed to be.'

Normally it's impolite to disturb a person's last resting place – rule number four: let the dead lie – but I'm sure Aunt Prunella wouldn't mind. You would be amazed at how little interest a ghost has in their former body. My body, as I have already explained, is floating somewhere in the river that runs through the woods and you don't hear me complaining about the little fishies nibbling on my fingertips or tickling my toes.

And so, under cover of darkness at the stroke of midnight (because that is the best time to dig up a corpse) Mildread, Maudelin and Jet met at the gravesite of Great Aunt Prunella and quietly, yet efficiently, dug up her bones. They were exactly where they were supposed to be.

Her skull still held the odd tuft of her thin, grey hair.

Her knitted shawl still clung to her bony shoulders.

Little black beetles and slimy grey worms slid between her false dentures and crawled out of her empty eye sockets.

'Resting peacefully,' said Mildread, replacing the dirt and giving the mound a satisfied thud with her shovel.

'Don't you-oo traipse that dirt through-oo the house,' moaned Aunt Prunella.

It felt like an eternity before something exciting finally happened but when it did, Jet was fit to burst.

The police knocked on the dilapidated door of Crow Cottage to question Birdy Black about the body in the blackberry bush. To date, no one had any idea who the corpse was and, quite frankly, the police were beginning to feel a little frustrated. Finding a body can be a rather exciting endeavour for a policeman. There's lots of activity going on, what with removing the body and forensic teams scouring all over the burial site with a fine tooth comb and then declaring the body a John or Jane Doe (that means they don't know who he or she is). After that, a full-scale investigation is given the go-ahead by HQ (Headquarters). Naturally this involves a lot of paperwork, and head scratching, and blackberry pie (to keep their energy levels high), and all that.

That was day one.

Now, however, they had hit a brick wall and, let me tell you, it wasn't pleasant. Not pleasant at all. Next came the legwork, and Constables Ray and Jay were not exactly in peak physical condition for such an undertaking. They would have preferred it if the case could be solved without having to go further than the Bellwether house – or Ground Zero as they called it – but, at a pinch, they'd settle for the hidden house next door even if it was a rather bedraggled-looking bungalow.

Birdy made them a cup of tea – no blackberry pie, I'm afraid – and Constables Ray and Jay got down to the nitty-gritty. Had either Birdy or Jet noticed anything unusual or untoward?

'Yes,' said Jet, she had. She'd hit a blood-plum over the hedge and it had hovered in mid-air for a split second; a clear indication that witchcraft was involved.

Constable Ray solemnly wrote it all down and thanked her for the information but then Jet saw him wink at Birdy and she knew what that meant. She scowled into her Sarsaparilla – a delicious brew made from the dried roots of various plants – and instead of wasting time trying to explain the ways of witches, she refused to say another word.

The constables, looking slightly relieved, quickly closed their notebooks and, like drunken sailors on a ship, they tottered over the uneven floorboards and out the door which slammed shut behind them, thanks to a sudden gust of wind.

Birdy rose creakily out of her chair and shuffled across the room. With great effort (and a fair amount of grunting) she reached up to a dusty, dark, leather-bound book on the top shelf. There were stains on the pages and bits of loose paper poking out and dried herbs squashed into the spine and on the cover scary-looking skull and crossbones – the universal sign for poison.

'Witchcraft you say?'

And Jet slowly nodded her head.

Leave no corner dark

I wish I could tell you what happened next but it's all a bit of a blur. The curtains at the kitchen window suddenly billowed out in a mad flurry, thunder rumbled across the mountains, the dark skies filled with streaks of lightning, the murderous crows flew up into the air above the woods, squawking and flapping their shiny, black wings and causing quite a commotion, and the sea began to swell and churn and toss the boats about, making it quite impossible to know which way to look. I call this 'distraction' and it is quite a useful tool when one wishes to keep one's affairs a secret. So, like I said, I wish I could tell you what happened in that crooked little cottage but I can't.

In due time, Jet ran outside and called Mildread and Maudelin over for an urgent consultation.

'We have to have a good look over that hedge,' she said, 'and find out what the witches are up to.

Birdy says they can shape shift into any animal they like.'

'Like a crow?'

'Yes,' said Jet. 'They can be anything they want to be. Isn't that terrific?'

I think it's safe to say that Jet's fascination with witchcraft had increased to the point where she no longer suspected that witches existed but now absolutely believed it. Furthermore, she believed, without a shadow of a doubt, that they were now living in the woods behind the hedgerow.

'Do you think there's more than one?' asked Maudelin.

'I don't know,' said Jet. 'That's something we'll have to find out. Are you with me?'

Mildread and Maudelin thought about this for a moment. Generally speaking, they had an open mind when it came to the unexplained, and the possibility of meeting a witch was clearly an opportunity not to be missed, but questions remained. Why were the witches so secretive? What did they have to hide? There's no denying the idea of witches in Wildwood appealed to their dark side but until they could decide for themselves, Mildread and Maudelin would have to rely on Jet to guide them and so, as a crow flew down onto the hedgerow and fixed them with a beady stare, the Bellwether twins nodded slowly in unison and Mildread said, 'We're with you, Jet,' and Maudelin added, 'Through thick and thin.'

First they tried peering through the thicket. But when they realised they couldn't see much, they began to climb the old plum tree; first Mildread, then Maudelin (because where one goes, the other follows), and finally Jet (last one up, first one down).

They lined up along the branch that stretched into Wildwood. They tried throwing leaves into a clearing but the wind carried them off in the opposite direction.

'They've put another spell on it,' said Jet, 'very crafty.'

'Why don't we just poke a stick at it?' suggested Mildread. She leant flat against the branch and waved a stick into the clearing.

'Careful,' said Jet. 'It might have a hidden hex that zaps right up the stick and…'

'Paralyses me,' finished Mildread.

She quivered her stick and her face went blank, her body rigid and stiff. To be fair, it wasn't all that different from her usual demeanour but Jet was highly attuned to the nuances of witchcraft and knew a hex when she saw one. She was just about to say so when Mildread threw the stick to the ground.

'Just kidding,' she said.

'You mustn't take risks like that,' admonished Jet. 'I might not be able to find the counter spell and then where would you be?'

'What would you do if I turned into a toad?'

'Nothing, it would be a major improvement,' said Jet.

'But if I was a toad then I'd give you warts.'

'All witches have warts. It's like a calling card.'

'So if we get warts, does that mean we'll be witches?'

'I guess so.' (Jet was rather pleased at this thought.)

'Then we'd know all about the witches in Wildwood.'

'Not really. Witches aren't friendly. They never show themselves to others.'

'Then what are we doing here if there's no chance of seeing one?'

'Waiting for them to slip up and catch them unawares.'

They sat on that branch for nearly an hour but nothing moved in Wildwood, nothing at all.

'I'm bored,' said Maudelin.

'Me, too,' said Mildread. 'Nothing is moving in Wildwood, nothing at all.'

'Don't you think that's strange?' said Jet. 'Where are the little animals foraging on the forest floor? Where are the birds flitting between the branches? Where are the insects crawling across the deadwood and daisies?'

'Where are the witches?' Mildread and Maudelin sighed in unison. 'Are you sure there are witches in these woods?'

'Don't lose your bottle now,' said Jet. 'What about all that sinister foreboding and malicious intent that Birdy keeps banging on about? There's a reason why we can't explore Wildwood and I aim to find out what it is.'

'Well you can do it without us,' said Mildread. 'We're going home for our tea.'

Olga was making borscht; a beetroot soup that looked like fermenting blood.

'Wait, I did see something in Wildwood. I swear to you on my mother's grave.'

'But Jet, you don't even know who your mother is. What if she's not dead?'

'She must be dead. Otherwise she would have turned up by now.'

'But why would she leave you on Birdy's doorstep?'

Good question. And it was one that Jet had pondered all her life. She was not ungrateful to Birdy for taking her in and raising her as her own, but why leave a baby on a doorstep in the first place? She did not like to think that she was unwanted. Better to believe that something awful had happened to her mother, and something unexplainable had happened to her father, and something incomprehensible had happened to all her other living relatives, and that the last thing any of them ever wanted to do was to abandon her on a stranger's doorstep without even a word of explanation.

'Well then I swear on my great, great, great, great grandmother's grave,' said Jet. 'She's bound to be dead by now.'

'What did you see?' asked Mildread, 'Tell us exactly what it was. Leave no corner dark, as Aunt Prunella would say.'

'It was a figure in black, wearing a cape made of feathers,' said Jet. 'It was hunched over and secretive and when it turned around to make sure it wasn't being followed, the feathers ruffled like a bird about to take flight.'

'Maybe that's all it was,' said Maudelin.

Wildwood was full of crows circling over the hooded trees, swooping down on their frightened prey, hiding amongst the thick foliage, or foraging beneath the roots and undergrowth.

'No, it was much too big to be a bird,' said Jet. 'And it moved too furtively to be a hiker in the woods. It was a figure in black with something to hide. And everyone knows that means it's a witch.'

'Honestly, Jet, you have a funny way of looking at things,' sighed Mildread. 'We're going home for our tea.'

'Do whatever you want,' said Jet. She threw a blood-plum into the wood, not so much to see if it would hover in mid-air but this time as a precaution.

If the witch had booby-trapped the forest floor then the purple plum, and not Jet, would suffer the consequences.

Suddenly, whether it was due to a trick of the light caused by a shadow falling over Wildwood or something much more sinister, the plum, in the blink of an eye, simply disappeared.

Here one moment, gone the next (as the Bellwethers would say).

And in that instant, there came the loud beating of heavy wings.

The girls nearly jumped out of their skin. Fantastically grotesque – jumping out of your skin – and probably not likely to really happen but that's certainly how it feels. When it came to the dark and mysterious Wildwood, there had always been a strange pull that led them to the hedgerow each and every time. It was almost like a magical siren was calling to them, beckoning them closer and inviting them in. Was it a trap? Or were there many wonders to be found deep within Wildwood?

If only Jet hadn't made that promise to Birdy. Still, she couldn't help thinking that Birdy would not have meant for her to ignore so many signs and so she swung herself down from the tree and stepped over the stile so that she had one foot on one side of the hedge and one foot on the other, much like a witch straddling a broom. She had no intention of entering

Wildwood just yet but surely a little pre-emptive peek wouldn't do anyone any harm? That's the thing about Jet. She was eager to see the unseen and know the unknown. If danger were to come knocking at her door, she would fling it open with a fearless curiosity and say, 'Who goes there?'

And this time was no different. She took a step over the stile and whispered into the gloom, 'Who goes there?' and as if in reply, the blood-plum rolled out from the shadows and winked at them.

It was like a red rag to a bull. Whatever was in there was daring her to take a step over the forbidden line and if there's one thing Jet could not resist, it was taking on a dare.

She didn't need to wait for anything else to happen. Quite frankly, a winking plum was enough to convince her that something dark and uncertain lurked deep within Wildwood. Naturally she was chomping at the bit to investigate further but right at the moment that Jet readied herself to leap into the abyss, Olga began to urgently call out, 'Girls! Girls! I need you here at once!' and Wildwood was quickly forgotten as all three girls ignored the winking plum, the dark shadows, the circling crows, the blackberry thorns, the ominous sky and the hornet's nest, and made a beeline back to the Bellwether house.

Things can happen in the blink of an eye

But the urgency in Olga's voice was a false alarm. When dealing with winking blood-plums and bodies buried beneath blackberry bushes, one tends to develop a heightened sense of urgency. Olga, on the other hand, dealt with crises in the kitchen. They tended to involve burning things to a crisp, or perhaps an accidental poisoning, or, in this case, sending the girls into town to replace pilfered offal.

I'll save you the trouble of looking that up in the dictionary for I'm fairly certain you won't have had any dealings with offal in your lifetime. If you have, then you have my sympathy. Offal is the rubbishy bits of a carcass and, believe me, it is awful. Pilfered offal means that someone has inexplicably stolen it. Most people are not that partial to the heart, liver or brain of a dead animal but I'm sure I don't have to explain to you why Mildread and Maudelin considered it a delicacy not to be missed. In this case, I'm afraid Miss Crawford agreed with them wholeheartedly and had thus decided to purloin the treasure from right under their noses.

Miss Crawford was a black crow that frequently made quite a nuisance of herself by hopping onto the kitchen windowsill, pecking at the glass and poking her head through an open window to steal whatever treats were laid out on the kitchen cabinet. She had a distinctive way of cocking her head to one side as if she understood every word you said and yet questioned your sanity.

The Bellwether twins had named her Miss Crawford because it means crow-foot. But she also bore an uncanny resemblance to a famous old movie star (now dead) called Joan Crawford. Both Miss Crawfords were fearsome, scary creatures not to be trifled with but only one of them had pilfered the offal and this time it was not the dead one causing all the trouble.

So Mildread and Maudelin set off into town in order to replace the offal and Jet, always ready for a new adventure, eagerly joined them.

There was not a lot to see in the tiny fishing village of Bitterly Bay but that was entirely the fault of the fog. It sat on the shoulders of the passers-by, drooped over rooftops, slid seductively down chimneys, floated over the waves, and made any vista instantly invisible. Sometimes you couldn't see the person right in front of you until you were almost nose to nose (which did away with any notion of being unsociable).

As Mildread, Maudelin and Jet bicycled down the hill, the grey fog was ever-present, the threat of storm as strong as ever, but visibility was a little better than expected. From the vantage point up high, the crows watched the girls cycle past a jetty, a telescope, a decommissioned canon, the skeletal remains of a monster whale, a half-submerged shipwreck, and a scattering of shops squeezed along the shoreline. And it was into The Abandoned Book Shop that they saw Jet disappear.

Mildread and Maudelin leant their bicycle against a lamppost out the front, then crossed the street and stepped into the butcher shop. But as they were going in, they smacked straight into Gideon Byrd coming out.

'Are you alright?' said Gideon, looking only at Maudelin.

It was as if Mildread didn't exist at all. That was fine with her for she had no interest in Gideon, either. In fact, she would have been perfectly happy to ignore him completely.

Maudelin, however, had the unfortunate habit of going weak at the knees whenever Gideon was near.

Mildread could never understand it.

'We'll be fine,' she said, irritably, 'if you will just get out of our way.'

Gideon scowled, as if noticing her for the first time. 'Do you have a brain injury, Mildread?' he snapped. 'Did you hit your head too hard smacking it against my collarbone?'

'That puny thing?' scoffed Mildread. 'I could snap it in two in the blink of an eye.'

She pushed past Gideon, and Maudelin had no choice but to follow her into the butcher shop because, as you well know, where one goes the other follows.

'I don't like the way you look at him,' said Mildread to Maudelin.

'Neither do I,' said Maudelin to Mildread, 'but I can't seem able to stop myself.'

Within minutes of the offal being purchased, the Bellwether twins found themselves standing back on the footpath out front, with a murder of crows for company. Most would find this unsettling. Mildread and Maudelin did not.

Maudelin (dare I say, hopefully) looked about for Gideon.

Mildread looked up at the broken lighthouse perched on the rocky outcrop of Wildend. All you could see of it was the top, poking through the swirling fog, but somehow it still managed to loom large over the township. Some saw it as a kindly figure watching over their loved ones. To others it looked forbidding and judgemental. Most would have said it was old and decrepit and dismiss it out of hand, but to Mildread's mind, it was a lonely sentinel standing guard over the town.

'It's a pity it's broken,' she said.

Maudelin, her thoughts still lingering on Gideon's collarbone, said, 'It is?'

'I wonder how it happened, a fearsome storm, perhaps,' said Mildread.

'More likely a vicious rugby match,' said Maudelin. 'What makes you think it's broken, anyhow?'

'I can see it.'

'You can?'

'Can't you? There's a gigantic crack running from the base all the way to the top.'

(There was indeed a massive crack down the side of the lighthouse; that's why it was broken.)

'I had no idea you were so interested,' said Maudelin.

'Well, I'm not as obsessed as Jet.'

'Jet is obsessed with Gideon's collarbone?'

'What are you talking about?' said Mildread crossly. 'No one on this planet is obsessed with Gideon's collarbone, except perhaps Gideon. I'm talking about the lighthouse.'

Maudelin blushed, hoping Mildread wasn't reading her thoughts right at that very moment. 'Oh, of course you are. Why do you think it's broken?'

'Something happened to it, I suppose. They say there was a monstrous storm one night and it got hit by lightning. I guess that's when that whale and shipwreck ended up here.'

She pointed at the wreckage littering the shoreline.

'I wonder why we don't remember it,' said Mildread.

It seemed as though these things had been there forever but no one quite knew when they had arrived. Surely it would have been reported in the local gazette but even if you were to spend an entire afternoon in the archives of the library, you would not find any mention of it. The ship had been a large vessel, carrying many passengers across the vast ocean but no names had ever been recorded, no obituaries posted, no mourners laying wreaths upon the shore.

And what about that whale? It had been almost as big as the ship. What on earth could have made it beach itself in the bay?

Naturally, people blamed the lighthouse. They assumed that when lightning struck, cleaving it in two, and plundering the bay into darkness, the ship and the whale were unable to keep from dashing against the rocks.

But, considering that the lighthouse no longer shone its beam out to the sea, it's a wonder more catastrophes had not befallen them.

These days, any wreckage found floating in the sea invariably wound up in The Shipwreck Shop. It was a tiny shop filled to bursting point with treasures dredged up from the bottom of the sea. Some things are better left buried, the Bellwethers would say (and as a general rule this is usually true), but in this case every child in Bitterly Bay would bitterly disagree.

To them, the Shipwreck Shop was a treasure-trove of hidden delights and the harder it was to unearth a treasure, the more the Bellwether twins loved it.

They paused for a peek but did not go inside, the stench of offal would have permeated the entire shop and they couldn't bear to sully such an exquisite space so they stood on the footpath out front and stared in the window at

- a bent tuba,
- a broken trumpet,
- a cracked plate,
- a chipped mug,
- a wooden mermaid once used as a ship's figurehead,
- a dented old diver's helmet,
- an old leather boot,
- a water-logged sea chest,
- a faded and torn treasure map,
- a paper crow in a shadow box,

- a rusty sword,
- a crumbling dagger,
- a pile of coins in various stages of decomposition,
- and a bag of blackened eyeballs.

At least I think they were eyeballs but I could be mistaken. Perhaps they were just an innocent bag of mouldy marbles.

Suddenly the girls realised that the one and only traffic light in town had changed to red and if they moved quickly enough they might possibly cross the entire street before the WALK sign flashed to DON'T WALK. But the vehicle idling impatiently at the light seemed to have other ideas.

As Mildread and Maudelin stepped off the kerb, the engine revved, the tyres squealed, and they both looked around in surprise as a van headed resolutely in their direction and their precious offal was lifted up into the air and over their heads as death came barrelling towards them.

Expect the unexpected

There was little traffic in Bitterly Bay. Except for a small black delivery van that sat at the dock and was only driven when absolutely necessary, most people preferred to walk or bike – less chance of a serious injury when ploughing into another through the fog, I suppose – so no one had quite figured out why there was a traffic light in the middle of Main Street.

I suspect the Mayor may have anticipated the possibility that this one delivery van could cause quite a bit of trouble if given carte blanche down Main Street.

Most of the shops were self-sustainable but anything extra was brought across the bay from the mainland by ferry and loaded onto the delivery van at the dock. It was, therefore, quite impossible to know who would be driving the van unless someone had ordered something very important and was waiting eagerly at the dock, hopping from one foot to the other, ready to leap into the driver's seat and go about their business in a brisk and timely fashion. Most of the time, no one was really in that much of a hurry. Sometimes the van would sit on the dock for half the day before somebody finally turned up. The only stipulation was that the driver be someone tall enough to see over the steering wheel. So that really only excluded Mrs Dimple from the teashop and children under ten.

As an extra precaution, though, the Mayor put in that traffic light. Unfortunately, most people in Bitterly Bay were rather casual about road rules. Sometimes your whole future can be decided in a split second by how quickly you deal with the unexpected. Have you ever noticed that?

Luckily for us, Mildread and Maudelin had excellent split-second decision-making abilities so when the van headed straight for them, each girl made a grab for the other's hand and flung their free hand out towards the oncoming vehicle and the strangest thing happened. It veered away, as if struck by a more powerful force, splashing puddles of muddy water across the windscreen and obscuring the face of the accursed driver.

The girls watched their offal fly through the air and land several feet down the road. One of them instinctively took a step back, and don't forget, where one goes, the other follows. And that's probably what saved them both from following in the footsteps of their awful offal.

The murderous van only narrowly missed them and, not surprisingly, kept going on its thoughtless way.

Maudelin's first thought was: *I hope Gideon didn't see that.* But he hadn't. He was, in fact, nowhere in sight.

Mildread's first thought was: *these boots are entirely inappropriate for being run-over by a heavy vehicle*. She then realised the absurdity of this thought. After all, a vehicle can do a lot more damage to a pedestrian than merely running over a foot.

Luckily the Bellwether twins were completely unharmed, save for a shaky disposition, and someone very kindly returned their slightly squashed offal so really it was no harm, no foul.

But someone on the other side of the road seemed to think otherwise. They were shrieking and flailing about, arms filled with a toppling stack of old books piled so high that you could not see their face. They were also carrying a fishing pole. It swayed so violently back and forth that the hook on the end threatened to poke each passer-by in the eye with every vigorous shake of the arm.

'You were nearly KILLED!' shouted an all-too-familiar voice.

One after the other, each book fell to the ground until the shrieking person's head emerged. It was Jet. She ran across the road, completely ignoring the DON'T WALK sign.

Mildread and Maudelin ducked down to avoid the swinging fishhook and tried to regain their composure but since they'd never really lost it, there was very little for them to do but to stare at Jet. She was panting heavily with eyes bugged out, arms still flailing, books still falling, and hook still swinging.

'What a calamity,' she breathed excitedly. She then stepped back onto the road, swung her rod high in the air, and attempted to flick the hook on the end towards the books scattered across the road.

'What are you doing, young one?' came a very cross voice from the other side of the road as Mrs Fossle emerged from the Fish & Bait shop on the corner and marched across the road towards the girls, picking up the old books along the way. Mr and Mrs Fossle were not only the owners of the Fish & Bait shop but also Gideon Byrd's grandparents.

'Mrs Fossle, leave them be,' urged Jet. 'I need to practice my book-hooking skills.'

'That is not a word,' said Mrs Fossle, but she looked a little unsure. English was not her first language. 'No loitering,' she continued. She knew for certain that was a word and she was most familiar with it. The English had adapted it from her native land. In Dutch it was 'loteren', and either way it meant the same thing; books did not belong on the road and neither did girls for that matter. Mrs Fossle had a fear of large objects and unruly mobs looming at her through the fog and so she thought it best to nip that sort of behaviour in the bud. Consequently, whenever a crowd congregated in the street, Mrs Fossle swiftly moved them on before they had a chance to linger or loiter or loom.

'Move along, Maudelin,' she commanded, 'and take your smelly package with you.'

'I'm Mildread.'

'No matter, you can move along, too. Shoo! Shoo!'

She ushered the Bellwether twins down the footpath but was forced to stop outside the teashop when Jet's line hooked onto the back of her jumper and began to pull the thread apart. Mildread and Maudelin opened the door and quickly backed away as Mrs Fossle twisted about in a tangle of fishing line and wool.

Mrs Dimple looked up from behind the counter, 'Tea?'

It was always best not to ask for coffee in Mrs Dimple's teashop. Somehow it always tasted stale and a little bitter. Her tea, however, was divine and she was especially adept at reading the leaves at the bottom of your cup and prophesising your future. Somehow it always involved purchasing more tea.

'Yes please,' the twins spoke in unison. 'Blackberry tea would be lovely.' They found a table and took a seat in front of a large window looking out at the dark, threatening sky. Miss Crawford flew down and rested upon the swinging sign above the shop, fixing them both with a beady stare. Within seconds Jet joined them, triumphantly holding her fishing pole aloft as the hook trailed behind her with a lump of green wool on the end. The books lay on the footpath outside, pages fluttering madly in the wind.

'What a beauty,' Jet exclaimed, her eyes shining bright. 'Mr Fossle said this rod could hook the clouds out of the sky and he's not wrong.'

To be fair, the clouds hung so low they almost touched your nose and I'm pretty sure Mr Fossle would not have meant for Jet to hook his wife's favourite knitted jumper just to prove his point.

'What do you need a fishing rod for?' asked Mildread.

'And why all the old books?' added Maudelin. She was itching to get her hands on Herman Melville's *Moby Dick*.

'Something's stopping us from stepping into Wildwood,' said Jet. 'I think the witches have put a charm on it and I'd bet my bootstraps that no matter how hard we try, we won't be able to step foot onto that forest floor. But I want that plum. They've put a charm on that, too. It's probably full of poison. And it's all the proof we'll need that there are witches in the woods. It was whilst I was in the bookshop, searching for inspiration on how to get my hands on that plum, that it hit me.'

'A book hit you?' asked Maudelin, somewhat surprised, for she had always believed that books were rather helpful things as opposed to harmful.

'No, a book didn't hit me,' explained Jet, 'an idea did. That's when I realised I could spear that plum with a fishing hook and then hoist it up from the ground and pop into my pocket.'

'But how do the books come into it?'

'Well, I've gotta practice on something, don't I?'

Genius, really, but fatally flawed when you think about it. The trouble with Jet keeping a safe distance from the shadows in Wildwood is that Mildread and Maudelin didn't really want to avoid the darkness at all. They were super keen to discover if Wildwood held the key to the secret of the body buried beneath the blackberry bush and, if anything, that near-miss with the murderous van had increased their thirst for the macabre. It had even begun to occur to Mildread (and therefore to Maudelin as well) that perhaps whoever was driving the van intentionally steered it into their path. Had they unwittingly unleashed a demon into their midst when they'd disturbed that sleeping corpse? How delicious!

At the very least they could discount Mrs Dimple being the reckless driver. Not only would she barely have been able to see over the dashboard of the van, but from the look of that steaming urn I'd say she was busy keeping scolding tea away from her paying customers.

Personally, I have always believed that when death comes knocking, it is far wiser to lock the door tight (and hide under the bed, for good measure), but I don't have to tell you how Mildread and Maudelin and Jet felt about that.

Mildread, still tingling at the possibility that something wicked had wound its way into their bay, stared out the window and allowed her thoughts to settle on the half-submerged wreckage on the shore. 'Such strange things;' she mused, 'a ship... a whale... a broken lighthouse... and a body beneath the blackberry bush....'

Without thinking, Mildread and Maudelin linked hands and absentmindedly moved objects about the table using just their mind. First the sugar bowl... then a napkin... then a spoon....

Their teacups began to rattle in their saucers and the milk jug took a few hops across the table before the girls realised that neither of them was moving it with their mind. A rumble overhead vibrated down the ceiling, through the walls, and over the floor, but it was not until it travelled up their legs and into the base of their spines that they realised it wasn't thunder.

All chatter stopped.

'It is just a little storm in a teacup,' Mrs Dimple twittered.

A few heads looked up as a BOOM! thundered overhead and the room shuddered, leaving everything slightly askew. Ceiling plaster rained down on the tables, chairs upended, light fittings creaked overhead, windows rattled, glasses shattered, the ground shook, and the rumble became a roar.

Maudelin's ears were ringing.

Dust rose up around them.

Mildread's eyes were stinging.

For one chilling moment everything hung in the air as if holding its breath until suddenly the building shuddered and creaked and moaned and the entire roof caved in.

From the corner of her eye, Maudelin could see a monstrous blur coming at her like a freight train.

Something awful will happen

Gideon Byrd flew across the room and reached Maudelin just seconds before the roof did. In a domino type effect, Maudelin fell to the ground, Gideon fell on Maudelin, and the roof collapsed onto Gideon. Actually, the roof fell on everyone... everyone, except Maudelin. Debris and dust filled the air. Maudelin could barely breathe. She was trapped beneath Gideon's body and it felt like a lead weight pushing all the air out of her lungs. She tried to grunt but it sounded more like a groan.

'Are you alright?'

'Yes, I'm just... fine.'

'Are there any bones broken?' Gideon squeezed her arm and Maudelin felt her legs go wobbly.

'Oh, give me a break,' said Mildread from beneath a nearby chair.

As Maudelin lay on the floor, the breath knocked out of her, she tried to work out if Gideon's plan was to save her or to squash her flat. Was he just in the right place at the right time? Or was he responsible for all this mayhem? Surely he wasn't so worried about her wellbeing that he'd been watching out for her from a distance, ready to pounce if trouble struck? Maudelin didn't quite know how to feel about this. Annoyed? Irritated? Insulted? Or perhaps, secretly thrilled?

Without another word Gideon helped her to her feet. She joined the others as they emerged from the rubble, dusting themselves off and congregating onto the footpath out front. Mr and Mrs Fossle appeared with blankets and water and soothing words of comfort (and Mrs Fossle did her best not to bustle). No one had died or was even seriously hurt (which was something short of a miracle considering a roof landed on them) but from the look on the twins' faces, I'd say several people came perilously close. Not that they would ever wish harm on another. But Mildread and Maudelin found a certain secret delight in being so close to death. Their faces developed what I like to call a locked-in look. To the outside eye nothing has changed – their mouths don't turn up at the edges, their faces remain grim and impassive – but you get the uncomfortable feeling that they are all lit up on the inside.

'You were nearly KILLED... again,' exclaimed Jet.

'We know,' they said. 'Isn't it delicious?'

'What do you mean by again?' asked Gideon. His face was the colour of his freckles.

Jet quickly told him all about the runaway van at the traffic light and how unfortunate it was that, once again, the Bellwether twins were in the wrong place at the wrong time.

But, as far as the twins were concerned, they were in exactly the right place at exactly the right time. A cold feeling of dread trickling down your spine is your body's way of telling you that you are in grave danger. As a rule, it usually means that something awful is about to happen. And right at that moment the Bellwether twins could feel that dread dripping down their spines bringing the threat of death ever closer to their door.

And they hugged that feeling tightly to their chests.

Mildread looked at Maudelin.

Maudelin looked at Mildread.

Mildread thought, *You could be next.*

Maudelin thought, *You, too.*

They frowned on the outside but smiled on the inside with that locked-in look.

Nobody else knew what to do because they had no idea, no idea at all, what the Bellwether twins were thinking, thanks to that grim expression on their faces.

Jet, however, had seen that look before and correctly guessed that they were thoroughly enjoying all this danger and intrigue. Although she, too, was drawn to danger, she had bigger fish to fry, so to speak. Her fishing rod was a little bent but otherwise in good working order so she scooped up her books and set off down the sidewalk.

'See you later,' she called out. 'I'll be at Wildwood, practising my flick!'

She meant, of course, that she would be gripping her fishing rod, flicking her wrist, and casting her line into the trees in the hope of snagging that purple plum with her hook. That's if the plum was still there.

And let's hope it was, for it must have been very important to Jet or else I'm sure she would not have passed up the opportunity to investigate a roof collapsing in a teashop. Those sorts of opportunities rarely come up and, in my opinion, are certainly not to be missed.

Mrs Dimple emerged from behind the counter and said, 'What happened?'

'The roof collapsed!' someone shouted from underneath the rubble.

'I can't think why it would do such a thing,' said Mrs Dimple, looking a little dazed.

'I think it was a bomb,' said Gideon.

'A bomb you say?'

'Yes, a bomb!'

Now how on earth would he know?

Mildread and Maudelin appeared to have lost their squashed meat again. At first this seemed to be their main concern ('Olga is going to kill us!') until Gideon rather accurately pointed out that it looked like someone else was trying to get to them first.

'But why?' he said. 'What have you done?'

Good question.

'Could it have anything to do with the body in the blackberry bush?' asked Mildread.

Nobody wanted to admit it but, standing amongst all that dust and debris and darkening skies, the possibility that something evil had crept into their town was as plain as the (dirty) noses on their (dusty) faces.

The rain held off (just) but it was still gloomy and grim. Constables Ray and Jay turned up and seemed completely baffled by the whole event but they were soon underway gathering evidence and talking to witnesses, helped along by Mrs Dimple's butternut biscuits (to keep energy levels high).

No one believed it could be a ruthless attack by reckless criminals, or a reckless attack by ruthless criminals for that matter. Not in Bitterly Bay. I doubt anyone vaguely resembling a ruthless (or reckless) criminal would have even heard of the place. Most people haven't. More likely some lunatic had blown up the café in retaliation for bad coffee. That sort of thing was quite common. Bitterly Bay was awash with lunatics.

Thunder rumbled overhead. Everyone rushed to put black plastic sheets over the gaping hole in the roof. Gideon seemed to be in the thick of it, talking to the police in a most earnest fashion, and it hadn't escaped the twins' attention that rather dangerous things had been happening to them ever since they ran into him.

He marched towards Maudelin with eyes ablaze, mouth set tight, and the bag of squashed offal in his hands. 'I don't care what anyone else says, I definitely think someone is trying to kill you,' he hotly declared.

'I knew it,' said Mildread, ignoring the fact that he was ignoring her. 'But how did you know it?'

There are two things about Gideon that everyone knows for a fact: his mother, Dottie, can be a little nutty at times and whenever something unspeakably thrilling happens, Gideon's freckles turn pink.

His face was now so ablaze that you could roast marshmallows off him.

'I think there's a lunatic on the loose,' he said, hoping fervently that this time it was not his mother.

Death will have its day

The wind picked up. It tugged at the tendrils of Mildred and Maudelin's hair. They watched the fishing boats bobbing in the bay and the black crows circling overhead as Mrs Fossle (not able to contain herself a moment longer) attempted to disperse the crowd.

'Move along, Mildread,' she commanded.

'I'm Maudelin.'

'Well, you can move along, too,' said Mrs Fossle, shooing them across the street.

They headed for The Abandoned Book Shop, where old, abandoned books were found a new home thanks to Mademoiselle Gabrielle who believed that tired old things were far more valuable because they had a story to tell. This would seem especially true of books, don't you think?

And the same can be said of Mademoiselle. She was seated just inside the doorway on an elegant, if slightly battered, old chair, looking about a hundred years old (Mademoiselle, not the chair – that looked much older).

'Such a big explosion,' Mademoiselle murmured in a thick French accent. 'My ears ring from zee bang.'

'Gideon Byrd thinks someone is trying to kill us,' said Maudelin

'Probably,' agreed Mademoiselle. 'I see zee runaway van chasing you over zee street and now you are almost crushed by zee tea. Once is coincidence. Two, I think not.'

Mademoiselle glanced over to where her one and only customer sat in shadow, hunched into one of the shop's reading chairs. It looked like they were trying desperately to blend into the wallpaper but then the Bellwethers (and their close proximity to death) frequently had that effect on people.

'So you do think we were the intended target?' asked Mildread.

'I only say it is possible,' said Mademoiselle. 'But then again, maybe someone has zee beef with Mrs Dimple.'

'Who would have a beef with Mrs Dimple?' said Maudelin. 'She's the sweetest lady in the world.'

'Not really,' said Mademoiselle darkly. 'She puts poison in zee tea.'

'It's called artificial sweetener.'

'That's not sugar! It is a crime and she should be locked up in zee prison.'

Mildread and Maudelin glanced at each other. Both had a clear vision of sweet, plump Mrs Dimple sitting in a jail cell in a sack dress made of artificial sweetener packs.

'You have to admit, it's not every day someone blows up the teashop,' said Mildread.

'Thank goodness for that!' cried Mademoiselle. 'Have I ever told you about zee French Revolution?'

I'm pretty sure she wasn't talking about first-hand experience. The French Revolution was in 1789. There's no way she could be that old. Is there?

'Maybe it's got something to do with that body we found buried beneath the blackberry bush,' said Mildread.

'Maybe,' murmured Mademoiselle.

'I think it does,' said Maudelin. 'I can feel it in my bones.'

'Oh, well, if you feel it in your bones then that is another matter,' said Mademoiselle.

But before she could ruminate further, Mrs Fossle was back. She seemed a little anxious that they were still lurking about in doorways. 'Are you going in or coming out?' she demanded.

'These are my nieces,' sniffed Mademoiselle, and I suppose they were, in a roundabout way.

Mademoiselle Gabrielle was a friend of their mother's. They met at a party in Paris.

Their mother was a bit of a gypsy, disappearing on another adventure whenever the wind changed direction and collecting lots of interesting and unusual artefacts along the way, which she sent back to Mildread and Maudelin to store in the cavernous attic alongside the ghost of Aunt Prunella. Aunt Prunella didn't seem to mind. More objects to dust, I suppose. Anyway, on one such expedition, their mother sent Mademoiselle home:

My darling girls,
Please find a nice spot
for this extra-special little French thing
that I just couldn't resist pocketing in Paris.
XX Mother

Mademoiselle arrived with jet beads sewn into the lining of her petticoat but the girls weren't exactly sure whether the extra-special little French thing was the beads or Mademoiselle. They very wisely decided not to store her in the attic. She had a lovely room under the eaves, overlooking the sea.

'And they are neither coming nor going,' added Mademoiselle after some thought.

'Neither coming nor going is neither here nor there,' declared Mrs Fossle. But she still looked cross that they were, once again, loitering in the street.

She was just about to say so when Mademoiselle looked up at the sky and closed one eye. 'Storm is coming,' she said.

Maudelin looked hopefully at the sky but Mildread was rather keen to get home to see if their father had begun to examine the corpse – had he tested for the possibility of poison yet, and what about the level of decay and rot? She would be so cross if he'd started without her.

As the Bellwethers liked to say, death will have its day and Mildread did not want it having its day without her.

She silently merged into the shadows and Maudelin followed because that's what they do. Presently, they emerged at the end of the street on their tandem bike. Tandem means one behind the other, which describes Mildread and Maudelin to a tee. But since Mildread usually takes the lead and Maudelin usually follows, it may explain why Mildread loathed their tandem bicycle and Maudelin did not. She'd sit on the back seat, legs tucked up out of the way of those pesky pedals, nose buried in a book, hair flying out behind her like the sails of a pirate ship, as Mildread gripped the handlebars, gritted her teeth and pumped her legs like mad. Sometimes it was hard to ride uphill, must be the aerodynamic pull that two pushbikes stuck together can create. Maudelin also couldn't understand why it took Mildread so long to pedal uphill. Clearly she was trying her hardest.

But, unbeknownst to both of them, as Mildread pumped her legs like mad and headed up the hill for home, someone was watching. Someone who knew that it would only be a matter of time before those Bellwether girls got what was coming to them.

The lone figure stepped away from the curious onlookers and headed for the rocky outcrop of Wildend.

It had started to rain. Mildread and Maudelin dismounted from their tandem bike because the rain was stabbing Mildread's face.

'You know, just once it wouldn't kill you to take the lead on this stupid bike.'

'Oh no,' said Maudelin. 'You're much better in front. I would be completely useless.'

'You're completely useless on the back, too, so I don't see what difference that would make,' Mildread huffed.

'Some are born to lead. Others are born to follow.'

'The trouble is, you were born to take advantage of a good thing,' said Mildread.

But, when you got right down to it, Maudelin was probably right. Mildread much preferred to make the decisions and to be the one out in front and if that meant she ended up doing all the legwork, then so be it.

She kept her head down and shouldered her way through the storm as they pushed the bike along the narrow track between clifftop and sea. Below them the waves crashed violently against the rocks. Their long capes billowed out behind them in the wind looking for all the world like wings and it really did look like they were about to take off and soar above the crashing waves.

Maybe that's why they were being followed.

And maybe that's why a hand reached out to grab hold of Maudelin.

Why should only the dead be miserable?

Maudelin twisted her body against the wind and kicked out with all her might. Her black leather lace up boot connected with a shin and a strangulated voice cried out, 'Ow!'

'Oh good grief, Gideon,' she moaned. 'I nearly pushed you off the cliff.'

'A wasted opportunity,' muffled Mildread into her cloak.

'It looked like you were about to fall,' said Gideon.

To be fair, the wind was buffeting them this way and that and the path they were on was quite perilous but Maudelin still couldn't be sure if Gideon reached out a hand to help or to hinder her.

'This weather is fit for neither man nor beast,' grumbled Gideon.

Yes, but which one are you? Maudelin thought to herself.

Who cares! Mildread thought back. (Don't forget they can read each other's mind.)

She opened the crooked wrought-iron gate into their yard and pushed their bike rather aggressively down the overgrown path. Maudelin, as usual, followed. There was no fence – most of the spikes had fallen into the sea or rusted into the earth – so it looked a little silly opening the gate when they could just as easily step around it, but certain things must always be done the proper way for it is the polite thing to do.

Halfway to the door, Maudelin turned back. 'Well, come on. We can't leave you out here now that you're injured.'

Gideon hobbled down the path towards them. It was a red letter day; the first time he had ever been invited into their home. He was both excited and terrified at the same time. He desperately wanted to see what the inside of their house looked like but, at the same time, he desperately wanted to make it back out alive.

He glanced up at the attic window. He couldn't be sure, what with the driving rain and the pain in his leg, but he thought he saw a pair of pale, sad eyes staring back at him.

'Are you sure it's alright? Your father won't mind?'

'He'll be in the basement with the dead body all afternoon,' said Maudelin. 'He won't even know you're here.'

Somehow that didn't exactly comfort him.

To Gideon's mind, the house resembled a gigantic bird squatting on the clifftop, ready to swoop down and devour its prey. But I think it looks more like a grand old dame, majestic in its decay, sitting resolutely on the edge of the coastline and refusing to topple into the sea regardless of the bitter winds and corrosive salt water. Much of the old grandeur is still evident. Its dilapidation just gives it more character and charm. At least that's what I think.

Gideon, however, was beginning to have his doubts the closer he came to the imposing front door. 'Look, I'm fine. Really I am.'

'What rot. You're scared, is what you are,' said Mildread.

Well, Gideon was having none of that. He squared his shoulders, set his jaw, and hobbled heroically through the door.

From somewhere in the darkened hallway there came a hollow laugh.

'That's just the old pipes,' said Maudelin, 'the wind rushing through them.'

Gideon was willing to believe this even if his chattering teeth and knocking knees were not.

Inside, the light was dim but Gideon could still make out faded wallpaper, an impossibly high ceiling, and a grand staircase. At the foot of it, leaning up against the wall, was a battered Egyptian sarcophagus (that's a coffin for a mummified corpse) with a note attached to it:

> *My darling girls,*
> *Here's a little trinket I found*
> *whilst camel-riding in the desert.*
> *Hope there's room for it in the attic!*
> *XX Mother*

Clearly there wasn't. But, generally speaking, if they left the heavy objects downstairs for long enough, they usually found themselves upstairs in the end. No one really knew how, but sometimes it's best not to look a gift horse in the mouth. And, heaven forbid, the day may actually come when that happens!

The girls led the way through a large doorway into a gloomy room, made darker by the storm clouds hovering outside the windows, flanked by heavy dark drapes, and surrounded by stuffed dead animals and rather imposing furniture. Gideon got the feeling he was slowly being suffocated.

Mildread turned on a lamp. The soft yellow glow was the only warmth in the room.

Maudelin settled into a seat in the bay window and, magically, a book appeared in her hand. Miss

Crawford perched upon the windowsill and watched Maudelin disappear into the pages of her book. More crows settled on the gate and called out through the fog as the sky blackened.

Gideon sat in a faded velvet armchair and began to examine his leg. He didn't want to look like a cry-baby but he wanted Maudelin to have some remorse for what she'd done and maybe feel like she owed him an apology. He winced (a little too dramatically, if you ask me) but Maudelin was engrossed in her book and missed the whole performance.

Mildread stood in the centre of the room, arms crossed. 'Do you need a doctor? Perhaps they'll need to amputate the leg,' she said dryly.

The bay window had a panoramic view of the ocean all the way across to the broken lighthouse. Lightning arced across the sky and hit the beacon with a shuddering crack. Gideon leapt to his feet, his so-called injury forgotten.

'Did you see that?'

Mildread, who had a direct view of the lighthouse, said, 'No.'

'See what?' said Maudelin, her eyes still glued to her book.

'Oh, never mind.'

Mildread was itching to disappear into the basement to see how her father's autopsy was progressing. She figured that since she'd found the body, she had a certain claim upon it and should, therefore, be informed of any progress. But Gideon needed watching, too. Why was he staring at Maudelin all the time? And why wasn't Maudelin telling him to *go away*?

Gideon watched as a black beetle scurried across the page of Maudelin's book. 'There's a bug on your book,' he said.

'Yes, I know,' said Maudelin. 'It's marking my place.' As she turned the page, the beetle dutifully followed.

'What if the book is accidentally shut? Won't he get squashed?'

'Possibly, but he will still be marking my spot,' said Maudelin.

All at once the front door flung open. The wind and rain and dead leaves entered the hallway, along with a huge bear. At least I think it was a bear.

'I'm home,' bellowed the bear, 'just back from teeing up an exhibition at Pixy Point and a burial at sea!' And suddenly a huge, bedraggled figure was looming in the doorway.

'This is Uncle Barnaby,' (not a bear) said Mildread.

He didn't usually shout so much but the storm was rather noisy and he was temporarily deafened. (Actually, Barnaby was rather deafened and he shouted all the time but he's a little sensitive about it so let's not mention it, okay?)

Uncle Barnaby was not really an undertaker. In truth he was a rather eccentric artist. He'd taken over an enormous room at the back of the house for his studio and it was filled, floor to ceiling, with canvases and paint and horsehair brushes and foul-smelling turps and rather grand and sombre portraits of animal heads on human bodies (magnificently clothed) or human heads on animal bodies (no clothing required). Barnaby was always covered in paint with stiff, startled brushes poking out of his pockets, and his hair sticking out in all directions and containing every colour under the sun. Uncle Barnaby was what you would call a colourful character (and a rather messy painter).

This, unfortunately, made him entirely unsuitable for the rather sombre task of undertaking so he was only really called into service (or, more precisely, his boat was) whenever someone required a burial at sea. It's terrific fun being buried at sea, especially if the waves are choppy. Mildread and Maudelin particularly liked it when all the mourners suffered from sea-sickness. Rule number ten: why should only the dead be miserable?

'Olga!' boomed Barnaby, shrugging out of his big, wet coat. 'We need hot chocolate for…'

'Me,' said Mildread.

'And me,' said Maudelin.

'Me, too,' added Gideon.

'And me,' came a muffled voice from a closed door, which we can take to be the basement and the voice to be their father.

'For five,' bellowed Barnaby, hanging his coat upon a hook and clomping down the hallway towards the kitchen.

'Don't worry,' said Maudelin. 'His bark is worse than his bite.'

But Gideon wasn't so sure. Already he was beginning to regret his decision to come inside. He secretly wondered if there was still time for him to make a hasty retreat.

But, unfortunately, unbeknownst to Gideon, that was no longer possible.

Misery loves company

Six people lived in this grand, old house, seven if you count Aunt Prunella (and, of course, they always did) and I think I can reliably pinpoint where everyone was the moment disaster struck. As I've explained, the ghost of Aunt Prunella lived in the attic at the very top of the house with a round window facing out to sea (that's where Gideon saw the face) and it's true she was obsessed with keeping a clean house (I think that's why her spirit could not rest) but she preferred to clean at midnight when the main rooms were empty and she could literally dust up a storm. She'd create a little tornado in the centre of each room then open a window to let the wind carry it out to sea. Once a passing albatross was sucked into the swirling dust particles and ended up in Antarctica. But, as I have already explained, the attic was the main space that she occupied and the window was where Gideon saw the face so I think we can safely assume that the ghost of Great Aunt Prunella was in the attic when disaster struck.

Mildread and Maudelin had decided to take Gideon down to the basement to get a better look at the body they'd found beneath the blackberry bush.

Mildread was expressing a keen interest in dissecting the decaying tissue, 'I'd love to get a piece of that flesh under my fingernails...'

And Gideon was swaying slightly in the doorway...

Maudelin was doing that incredible thing readers do of being able to walk with nose planted in a book...

Their father was still locked away in the basement with the body...

Olga was in the kitchen...

Barnaby stomping down the hallway...

And Mademoiselle was still sitting just inside the doorway of The Abandoned Book Shop in the main street of Bitterly Bay...

And it was right at that precise moment that the unthinkable happened (for the second time that day).

It began with a loud and distant rumble, more ground-shaking and glass-rattling, and I'm pretty sure Gideon was all set to leap onto Maudelin again when quite suddenly an almighty BOOM! stopped everyone and everything in its tracks. I suppose when you live on the side of a cliff, perched precariously close to the edge, you are subconsciously bracing yourself for its inevitable collapse. So much so that when you actually hear it happen, your subconscious reacts before your conscious brain has even had a chance to work out what is happening. Perhaps that explains why, this time, Maudelin flung herself onto Gideon. I'm sure if you were to put this theory to her in just such a way, she would heartily agree that it was a desire to save Gideon from encroaching doom that propelled her so forcefully into his arms, and not for any other reason than that.

He certainly appreciated the gesture, even though he was apparently in no danger.

A large chunk of the clifftop broke away and fell into the sea but the house and everyone in it was safe. It was far enough away to escape any damage but close enough to feel the shockwaves.

Once everyone had recovered their composure, some more quickly than others (and, yes Maudelin, I'm looking at you), they made their way out front to assess the damage. Half the pathway had fallen into the sea.

'Well, it looks like you're stuck here,' said Mildread and Gideon felt the ground fall away beneath him. Wasn't he just moments ago wondering if he would ever leave?

'People will notice I'm missing,' he said.

'Well of course they will,' said Uncle Barnaby. 'We'll telephone your family and let them know you're safe.'

Gideon thought that was rather optimistic but he hoped for the best all the same.

'Thanks for trying to save me,' he whispered to Maudelin.

'I wasn't trying to save you,' Maudelin blushed. 'I lost my footing and fell. That's all.'

'Oh, well then I'm glad I could cushion your fall.'

Birdy was the first to reach the clifftop along with the murderous crows but there was nothing that could be done. Her face was covered in dirt, and leaves and twigs were stuck in her hair. Clearly she'd reached the edge before the debris had fully settled into the sea. Jet appeared from behind Crow Cottage, her hair looking wilder than a bird's nest and covered in leaves and twigs, but the twins figured that was probably due to the plum tree at the edge of the wood. No doubt she was still trying to hook that juicy blood plum from the forest floor.

'Mildread! Maudelin!' she gasped, 'You were nearly...'

But before she could say KILLED, they cut her off at the pass, and I mean that literally. They stood in front of her as she raced to cliff's edge and Maudelin said firmly, 'No, we weren't.'

'I cushioned her fall,' said Gideon helpfully.

The ghost of Great Aunt Prunella weaved between everyone, moaning pitifully like a good ghost should but not with the intent to frighten anyone. She was merely moaning at the dusty mess the clifftop collapse had caused.

Gideon gave an involuntary shiver. He still couldn't see or hear Aunt Prunella but he could feel the coldness in his bones and could hear the eerie moaning of the wind whipping about the clifftop.

'This is creepy,' he said.

Everyone assumed he was referring to the gigantic gaping hole in the side of the cliff. Tree trunks had been ripped from the earth, their roots forlornly exposed. The Bellwethers stared at the chasm with an air of indifference. Mildread and Maudelin had that locked-in look on their faces again and I am sure they were leaning into that feeling of dread and letting all that misery and woe wash over them like a warm, wet wave.

That is, after all, what the Bellwethers do best.

But, like I said, there was nothing anyone could do so Birdy went back to her garden and the others trooped back inside the Bellwether house, walking one behind the other like a funeral procession with Gideon reluctantly following in their wake and the ghost of Aunt Prunella bringing up the rear.

The crows circled over the clifftop, cawing eerily into the gloom.

Everyone gathered around the kitchen table for some nourishing hot chocolate. I imagine you would expect Olga to open the pantry and retrieve a packet of drinking chocolate, purchased from the supermarket, but that is not how proper cooks do it and certainly not how proper Russian cooks do it. It is not unheard of for a Russian to put Vodka in their chocolate but Olga just made hers the old-fashioned way, on the stovetop and so thick that you needed a spoon to consume it. Except for Miss Crawford, who liked to peck at the delicious, gloopy blob from a saucer on the counter.

Olga made the hot chocolate and put a saucer out on the windowsill for Miss Crawford, who dutifully swept down for her delectable treat.

'Another near miss,' said Mildread. 'This is getting to be a habit. It's starting to look like somebody wants the whole town dead.'

And in a way she was right. Bitterly Bay was a tiny community full of strange and interesting characters. Enough to fill a book, some would say. (At least that's what I'm hoping!) Its rich history was full of feuding factions and suspicious sabotage and the Bellwethers seemed to always be lingering around the edges. Not actually involved in any skulduggery, but not entirely innocent, either. And several of the Bellwethers had disappeared in rather mysterious circumstances.

Mildread was thinking, *Could one of them be the body found beneath the blackberry bush?*

And Maudelin was thinking, *Could it be Aunt Emily?*

When Uncle Barnaby said, almost to himself, 'My wife drowned in those waters.'

Mildread and Maudelin gave a start. Had he just been able to read their minds? It's not entirely unfeasible, I suppose. There were a lot of twins in the Bellwether family besides Mildread with Maudelin. There was their grandmother, Prudence, with Aunt Prunella; their mother, Elizabeth, with Aunt Emily; and their father, Byron, with Uncle Barnaby. It's likely they could all read each other's thoughts if need be. And, if further needs arose, you just might find that Uncle Barnaby could anticipate the direction that Mildread and Maudelin's thoughts were heading in and, as such, might happen to say at just the right moment, 'My wife drowned in those waters.'

'It's understandable that you're thinking of her now,' their father said. No doubt he was thinking the exact same thing. 'I guess we'll never know if dear Emily fell or jumped off that cliff but certainly a piece of the clifftop falling into those mysterious waters would get you thinking about her again.'

When Aunt Emily disappeared from the clifftop at Wildend, never to be seen again, Barnaby was missing at sea, presumed drowned. Rumour has it that Mildread and Maudelin's mother refused to believe that her sister was dead and so set off across the sea in search of her. They say that as her boat chugged out to sea, another boat, this one battered and broken and barely staying afloat, limped its way into the Bay and Uncle Barnaby, with a beard so long it brushed upon his knees, poked his head out of the cabin and barked, 'I'm back!'

Alas, he was too late. Aunt Emily was gone.

Uncle Barnaby looked very sad and the bark went out of his bluster. It must have been quite a shock for him to have finally returned from being lost at sea, having spent many years eating only raw fish and seaweed, and clinging to the hope that someday he would reunite with his true love, only to discover that she, too, was lost at sea, never to return.

The room went quiet, each person around the table lost in their own private thoughts. Only, perhaps, they weren't as private as they thought.

Gideon had the uncomfortable feeling that a lot was being said in that silence. He could feel a thickness in the air, as if arguments or emotions were being relayed through the quietness. He glanced nervously around the table but he couldn't for the life of him work out what was not being said.

'Penny for your thoughts,' he whispered to Maudelin.

'I was just wondering if the body beneath the blackberry bush could be Aunt Emily,' said

Maudelin, quietly. 'Perhaps she didn't fall off the cliff, but was buried in our garden.'

'Why go dragging all that up again?' moaned Barnaby.

'Things have been a little weird,' said Mildread, 'ever since we...'

She was about to say, ever since they bumped into Gideon outside the butcher shop but Maudelin interjected with, 'found the body beneath the blackberry bush.'

Beneath the table, she gave Mildread's arm a particularly painful pinch.

'First was the body, then the witches and then Gideon,' she hissed through clenched teeth.

'What witches?' demanded Uncle Barnaby. 'What in blazes is going on around here?'

'Nothing,' said Jet, giving Maudelin a swift kick under the table.

Mildread rubbed her arm (from the pinch) and Maudelin rubbed her leg (from the kick).

'This might be a little painful for some...' their father speculated, (it certainly was to Mildread and Maudelin!) '...but perhaps these uncanny events are all connected. It makes you wonder, doesn't it, what's going to happen next.'

Beware of things that go bump in the night

What happened next was dinner. Gideon telephoned home, resigned to the fact that a new path could not be dug until morning. They would have to cut into Wildwood and no one wanted to do that in the pitch dark.

Gideon wasn't exactly expecting a normal, dull dinner, but he was still a little surprised at a few strange things going on around him at the dinner table. For example, Mildread and Maudelin, who were practically inseparable most of the time, did not sit beside each other at the table. There was an empty seat between them with an empty plate on the table and an empty glass beside it.

'Who sits there?' he asked.

'Our mother does.'

'Where is she?'

'Nobody knows.'

'If she's not here then why leave a place for her?'

'In case she is.'

'Is what?'

'Here.'

'But she's not, is she?'

'No.'

(Not a very illuminating conversation, I must admit.)

Maudelin was once again reading a book, which Gideon had been told was rude but her father was also reading (a gruesomely illustrated encyclopaedia of anatomy) so Gideon figured it was probably allowed at this table. Olga had cooked an offal and cabbage stew with dumplings. Miss Crawford pecked frantically at the kitchen window. Gideon piled his plate with dumplings.

Uncle Barnaby propped a photo up against the salt shaker.

'Who's that?' asked Gideon.

'That's Aunt Emily,' said Maudelin. 'Just because she doesn't live here anymore doesn't mean she can't join us for dinner.'

This is a very strange family, thought Gideon.

And things were about to get even stranger when he was eventually given a bed to sleep in for the night. Since he couldn't get out, thanks to the clifftop falling into the sea, it stands to reason that no one else could get in, so Mademoiselle was forced to sleep elsewhere that night. Consequently, her bed was free. So Gideon was placed in it. He found himself in a tiny bedroom, tucked under the eaves. The dim lamp cast dark shadows on the faded floral wallpaper and distorted the portraits of cranky-looking people on the wall. There was a squeaky, wrought-iron bed with peacock feathers draped over the headboard and a heavy, overstuffed eiderdown with a spidery black lace coverlet atop the bed. Musky perfume lingered in the air. A milky crystal ball swirled ominously on the bedside table. There was the sound of eerie moaning overhead and creaking floorboards underneath.

Poor Gideon had the uncomfortable feeling that he was being watched and at one point he was sure he could feel breathing down the back of his neck. But he dared not open his eyes to check. Who knows what he might have found staring down upon him.

Outside the window, the waves crashed angrily against the rocks and Gideon was convinced that the rest of the cliff, including this house and the broken lighthouse, was about to crumble into the sea at any moment. He spent a tense, restless night bracing for impact. All through the night he heard a persistent tap-tap-tapping sound as if a bird were rapping its beak upon the glass, although why any creature would wish to get *into* this house was a mystery to him.

After hours of tossing and turning and sneezing and suffocating and bracing for impact and screwing up his eyes tight, Gideon finally threw in the towel, or in this case the eiderdown. He flung the bedclothes over his head and tried to shut everything out, and possibly earn himself a few minutes kip, when suddenly he heard the door creak open and soft footsteps creep across the room, and the bedding over his head was gently drawn back and, with his eyes still shut tight, he felt a tiny tap upon the freckle in the middle of his forehead...

'Aargh!' he hollered, throwing back the bedsheets and leaping to his knees in a ferocious fighting pose. They may have got him but he was gonna go down fighting!

Don't rock the boat

'Goodness, Gideon, is that how you always greet others in the morning?'

Gideon opened his eyes wide to find Maudelin standing in front of him in dressing gown and slippers.

'Sorry. I'm a little jumpy.'

'So I see. Breakfast is ready. Try not to attack the toast.'

Gideon could well understand why breakfast was considered the most important meal of the day. It seemed to be the time when this family sorted out their priorities for the day. Uncle Barnaby was heading over to Pixy Point to put the finishing touches on his exhibition and to pick up a body for burial at sea, but first a new path needed to be dug through the forest of trees. It was agreed that all hands on deck would build the road quicker so everyone gathered up some digging tools and headed out to the clifftop. As usual, Jet was one step ahead of them. She had begun the dig with a strange-looking tool that Birdy had fashioned for her. Birdy was deep within the thicket, determined to carefully remove precious plants and replant them in a safer spot before the new path destroyed them. Even the crows pitched in, swooping down and collecting debris along the pathway.

'Have you managed to retrieve that plum yet?' asked Mildread.

'No,' said Jet, looking intently at her long-handled digging and scooping tool. 'But I have a new idea…'

As they toiled, Uncle Barnaby went into great detail about his upcoming exhibition until all were keen to join him in Pixy Point just as soon as a new path had been cleared. Uncle Barnaby's battered and broken boat had been lovingly repaired and although a passenger ferry could easily commute to the mainland twice daily if required, most of the locals preferred to wait for Barnaby to ferry them across to Pixy Point, whenever that may be. I once heard that Mrs Dimple waited a full month for a chiropodist's appointment to remove a bunion on her foot because Barnaby had dry docked his boat to scrape barnacles off the bottom.

I'm not sure everyone would have fitted comfortably in the boat for the journey across the bay, but it wasn't an issue in the end. They say children have short attention spans but if you ask me, it's adults who are the more easily distracted. By the time the path was ready to traverse, Olga had returned to the kitchen, Birdy to her garden, and Mildread and Maudelin's father had locked himself in the basement with a pot of tea and a plate of crumpets (and the illustrated encyclopaedia of anatomy).

That left Mildread, Maudelin, Jet and Gideon to accompany Uncle Barnaby to Pixy Point. Gideon wasn't exactly sure why it was absolutely necessary for him to go, too, but it seemed to matter greatly to Uncle Barnaby that a male perspective be present at the gallery. Or was it the burial?

So, with a narrow path cleared through the wood and a murder of crows for company, the quintet headed down towards the jetty where the boat bobbed gently up and down in the water, waiting patiently for its next adventure on the waves.

As they walked down the hill, they passed the postman struggling up it on his bicycle, the back weighed down by an enormous wooden crate with lots of postage labels stuck on it. Another artefact from mother dearest, no doubt.

'I wish she would find smaller objects to send back home,' he puffed.

There was a round hole in the box, just big enough for an eye to peer through but Gideon made a conscious effort not to look at it. He didn't want to come face to face with an eye peering out.

When they reached the boat, he insisted on a thorough search of the hull. 'No more surprises,' he said. The crows hovered overhead, occasionally bursting through the grey clouds with a sudden 'Caw!' and setting everyone's nerves on edge.

As the boat pulled away from the shore, there came a frantic shout from the jetty. Gideon poked his head out of the cabin as they headed out to sea but whoever it was had a big floppy hat obscuring her face and whatever she was shouting was snatched up by the wind and carried off in the opposite direction.

'Just a lunatic trying to stop the boat,' he said, fervently hoping it was not his mother. He looked out at the choppy waters and tried not to think about the runny eggs he'd had for breakfast.

Uncle Barnaby stood above him, staring out to sea towards the Point. The waves grew choppier and the boat rocked from side to side.

Gideon tried not to think of the kippers he'd had with his runny eggs for breakfast. Kippers, I have to tell you, are just about the smelliest fish you can ever eat. Sometimes the memory of a kipper can last for days. He pressed his lips tightly together and slumped down in his seat.

Maudelin buried her nose in a book.

'I should have brought my fishing rod,' said Jet.

Mildread looked out the window. 'There's something in the water,' she said.

'Is it a shark? Now I really wish I'd brought my fishing rod.'

'No. It looks like a mermaid.'

A branch wrapped in seaweed floated by.

It looked like that might easily be the most interesting part of the voyage when suddenly, without warning, several popping sounds rang out above the usual sputtering of the engine. Smoke billowed out of the stern and the crows began to caw and circle Uncle Barnaby's head. The boat listed dangerously to one side and then to the other.

'Don't rock the boat,' groaned Gideon.

Maudelin scowled into the pages of her book. Mildread turned away from the window. Jet sat up straight and swivelled her head from side to side. And everyone held their breath.

Then, unbelievably, the boat began to sink. Slowly at first, then the dirty water churned around their ankles and began to suck them under. The sky suddenly turned very dark. Mildread and Maudelin quickly linked hands and the same thought echoed through their minds…

We can't swim.

But neither of them seemed particularly bothered by this.

Jet, on the other hand, was a magnificent swimmer thanks to Birdy Black. Not only was Birdy cautious when it came to the deep, dark wood, but she also feared the deep, dark sea. I suppose she could have made Jet swear to never go out in the water but since they lived on an island surrounded by the stuff, she'd decided, instead, to teach her how to swim.

The instant the boat began to sink Jet did a graceful dive into the ocean and with one powerful arm stroke after another, swam safely to the shore before realising that the others were not following. She could see Uncle Barnaby floating upon the water's surface like a cork in a bottle. She grabbed a rope from the jetty and threw it at him and managed to tow him to the water's edge, watched by the ever present black crows.

She then looked around for the others. Where were they?

Gideon grabbed hold of Maudelin's arm and pulled as hard as he could. I don't know if you know this, but wet clothing can be extremely heavy and it's very hard to pull another person out of a sinking vessel, especially when you're feeling extremely green around the gills… and the other person is holding on to another drowning person.

'You have to let go,' he gasped.

But that's the last thing that Maudelin wanted to do. She wanted to go down with the ship, or at least halfway down, and Mildread wanted to go down with her. Hand in hand, as always. But Gideon's grip on Maudelin was stronger than Mildread's. He pulled hard and the girls felt their fingers slide apart.

Mildread slowly sank down into the depths of the cold, black sea with eyes wide open and a calm expression on her face.

As Maudelin's head broke the surface, thunder rumbled like a freight train roaring through a tunnel. Maudelin's face was as dark as the sky and sea.

I feel I should point out at this stage, that neither Mildread nor Maudelin had a death wish. They just wanted to get as close to death as they could without actually dying. Have you ever heard the saying that you never feel more alive than when you're closest to death? Well, I don't recommend you try it. I have had many conversations with corpses who ruefully admit that they may have gone a little too far.

Underneath the waves, Mildread could hear nothing. Water rushed into her ears and mouth. She thought she heard Maudelin calling her name from very far away but then the blackness all around slowly shut her out and Mildread was alone in the dark.

Well, not quite alone.

Something long and slimy brushed past her legs. It felt much too big to be a fish. It whooshed past her head and arched its body around her.

As it swam past her face, she reached out and grabbed hold of a gill, or a fin, or a hump, or whatever on earth it was. For some reason the first thought that popped into her head was of that monster whale skeleton in the bay and from there she began to imagine the impossible, like the six-foot Coelacanth (pronounced see-le-kanth), thought to be extinct for 65 million years, or that elusive sea serpent, the Loch Ness Monster.

But whatever this creature was, she was hoping it would break the surface and show its face today.

Keep your enemies close

When Mildread opened her eyes a feeling of dread washed over her (how delicious!) but she was dry and she could breathe so she knew she was no longer in the water. She was lying on a bed in the doctor's clinic and sitting beside her was Maudelin. They reached out their hands and as soon as they touched, Mildread felt whole again. And, of course, Maudelin felt it too.

And every small object in the room rose up a tiny bit into the air.

Miss Crawford appeared at the window and watched the girls intently. She tilted her head to one side, ruffled her feathers and gave a tap or two on the glass.

'Right as rain,' whispered Mildread.

A nurse bustled in to check their vital signs. 'You both have stitches in your forehead, in exactly the same spot,' she said. 'And, Mildread, you have bruising down your left side.'

'I'm Maudelin.'

'Oh. You have bruising down your right side then.' She turned to Mildread. 'And you have bruising down your left. Well, what do you know; you're a complete mirror image of each other.'

Mildread was still trying to get her bearings when Uncle Barnaby barrelled in, leaving a nervous receptionist in his wake.

'Where's the doctor?' he demanded.

'Uncle Barnaby, we're fine,' said the girls but their voices sounded small and he was clearly not going to take their word for it. An expert opinion was what Barnaby wanted and the receptionist ran off to fetch a higher authority. The girls secretly hoped she wouldn't have the sense to alert security whilst she was at it.

'No overstimulation,' urged the nurse but Uncle Barnaby paid no attention to her, either.

'These are my nieces,' he boomed, 'and I want to know that they're alright!' A rather harried-looking doctor hurried into the room and tried to regain control but Barnaby was having none of it. 'What's the prognosis?' he demanded.

'They nearly drowned,' said the doctor. 'And they both have a rather nasty cut on their foreheads. Still, we expect a full recovery. They are very lucky to be alive.'

'Huh!' snorted Barnaby. 'There are worse things to be than dead,' he said, 'and personally I would consider it an honour to go down with the ship.'

The others looked a little confused. Surely he wasn't referring to that dinky little boat of his as a ship?

But Uncle Barnaby sailed on (so to speak). 'How long do they need to stay here?' he demanded.

'If there's someone who can look after them, they can go home today,' said the doctor.

Normally he would have insisted on overnight observation and that can be quite a comfort to people who've faced death square in the eye but everyone knows the Bellwether family (and especially Mildread and Maudelin) can savour a near-death experience for days (maybe even years). Rather than find it off-putting or scary, they actually welcome the sensation of almost being killed. And so the doctor was more than happy for the Bellwether twins to be released.

Just between you and me, I think he was rather relieved to see the back of them.

'Good,' Barnaby sighed, and suddenly all of the bark went out of his bite. He didn't want to be a gruff, old bear and he knew he'd been terrifying the staff but when Uncle Barnaby gets a bee in his bonnet, the best thing to do is to leave him be (or is that bee?). At least until he's gotten the gruff all out of his system. And now... well, now he had some fences to mend.

Not to mention a body to bury. Don't forget, he still had a burial at sea to organise. He thought that perhaps he could get the main passenger ferry to bring the body over from Pixy Point but he wasn't sure if the other passengers might go a bit wobbly over a corpse. It's not as if the dead body would be propped up on a seat beside them, but all the same Uncle Barnaby knew that the living had a little trouble coping with the dead although he couldn't figure out why. Hadn't he and his nieces just gone through a near-death experience? And you didn't hear them getting all squeamish about it. I suppose an undertaker would have a rather philosophical view of death.

And so, with a few loose ends to tie up, Uncle Barnaby turned to leave, bumping straight into Gideon Byrd in the doorway. Why was that boy always lingering in doorways and bumping into people?

Jet squeezed her way through and said, 'Aren't you going to tell them that Mademoiselle is in jail?'

'What?' Mildread stood up so fast she almost fell over. 'What happened?'

'Oh, yes, that,' said Uncle Barnaby. 'It seems the daft old woman had what she calls a premonition and tried to stop us before we headed across the Bay. She said she had a vision the boat would sink.'

Mildread and Maudelin cast their minds back to Gideon's comment at the jetty about a lunatic shouting incoherently as they left the shore. They should have known it was Mademoiselle.

'Apparently she legged it to the police station and was babbling on about a tragedy at sea when they received the news that our boat had indeed just sunk,' said Uncle Barnaby. 'Naturally they arrested her on the spot.'

'You have to do something. You have to get her out.'

'Don't worry; your father's trying to spring her as we speak. I'm sure it won't take long for the police to realise that she's not a terrorist but just a slightly batty bohemian with fortune-telling abilities. Now, your father's left us the hearse so let's get you kids home.'

He took off at a trot, or as fast as his bulk would allow, and the others did their best to keep up.

'It had to be a bomb on that boat,' said Gideon. 'I heard a bang, didn't you?'

'You and your bombs,' Mildread sighed.

'We must get to the bottom of this,' said Jet. 'There are far too many coincidences for my liking.'

'Speaking of getting to the bottom,' said Mildread, 'do you have any idea what's down there at the bottom of the bay?'

'Oh no, you didn't find another dead body, did you?'

'Better than that.'

'What could be better than that?' asked Maudelin.

'I found a sea serpent or, more precisely, it found me. It saved me. I think there's a prehistoric monster lurking down there and we have to find it.'

'Not another mystery to solve.'

'They're adding up, aren't they, one strange event after another.'

And what about Gideon, Mildread thought, knowing full well that Maudelin could read her thoughts.

Once again he was right in the thick of things. But did he really try to save them or was it his plan all along to let them drown? He did, after all, have a fascination for bombs and instead of checking the hull he could have been planting one down there.

Maudelin glared at Mildread, then turned to Gideon and said, 'Thanks for helping us again.'

'If it's alright with you, I think I'll hang around for a bit longer,' said Gideon.

He was not sure why he wanted to do this but every time he thought of Maudelin being in grave danger, he felt a protective instinct surge inside his chest.

'You'll get no argument from me,' said Mildread. She was still not sure if Gideon was the hero or the villain of this piece but you know that adage: keep your friends close and your enemies closer. She planned to be watching every move he made.

And besides, Maudelin was becoming rather attached to Gideon and that needed watching, too.

Don't hold your breath

U ncle Barnaby dropped them off at Wildend and returned to the police station and everyone eagerly awaited Mademoiselle's return.

But she was not the first to arrive.

Someone knocked hard and heavy at the door. Olga walked quickly down the hallway, wiping her floury hands on her pinny and opened the door with a curt and crisp, 'Yes? Who is banging on the door?'

'Mr Blatherskite, Transport Accident Investigator.' And a short man with oversized spectacles and bulging briefcase stepped into the hall.

It was a little crowded what with the hat hooks, the coat rack, the umbrella barrel, the gumboots, the Russian cook, four kids, and Miss Crawford flapping and squawking about his head, but Mr Blatherskite zeroed in precisely on his prey.

'Ah, there you are. You must be Mildread Bellwether,' he said to Maudelin.

'Yes,' Maudelin sighed, stopping herself from rolling her eyes just in the nick of time.

'And I'm Maudelin Bellwether,' said Mildread.

Jet and Gideon exchanged knowing glances because anyone who truly knew Mildread and Maudelin could easily tell them apart. And if you were a little unsure, you simply looked for the book in Maudelin's hand.

Olga ushered everyone into the sitting room (except for Miss Crawford who was unceremoniously given the boot). Mildread and Maudelin took a seat in front of Mr Blatherskite on the horsehair settee, Gideon found his favourite armchair and Jet grabbed the window seat (with Miss Crawford settling on the windowsill outside).

Mr Blatherskite took one look at the horrible gash across the twins' foreheads and said, 'I imagine you will be suing for disfigurement.'

'Will we?'

Up to this moment Mildread and Maudelin had no idea they were disfigured. They thought it was only a flesh wound, nothing too serious. No babies had wept or delicate women fainted. Were they now so hideously deformed that they would have to spend the rest of their lives hidden away in the attic? No doubt that would put a crimp in Aunt Prunella's plans.

Who was this rude and arrogant man?

'Perhaps you didn't hear me. I am Mr Blatherskite, Transport Accident Investigator. I'm here to find out what happened with your uncle's boat.'

Olga brought in a tea-tray and Mr Blatherskite attempted to balance a cup of tea on his knee whilst simultaneously rifling through a thick folder of paperwork. A few drops of tea splattered on his trouser leg and one large spot fell to the floor but nobody took any notice. Not even when the spot miraculously disappeared from the rug, like invisible ink on a page.

The Bellwether twins sat with their hands in their laps and a detached expression on their (horribly disfigured) faces. They weren't entirely sure they were ready to be interrogated by this obnoxious man but they were not about to let him intimidate them. If anything, having two identical girls, dressed in black with sombre expressions on their (hideously) scarred faces was a little intimidating in itself but, again, Mr Blatherskite was not the type to let such tactics affect him. It reminds me of a chess game where each player tries to overpower the other by the sheer force of their will.

Gideon sat rather awkwardly in his chair. He didn't like dainty teacups with delicate saucers. Mr Blatherskite looked up from his papers and gave him a decidedly unfavourable appraisal.

'I'm sorry, is it absolutely necessary for you to be here?'

Gideon didn't budge.

'Who exactly are you?' asked Mr Blatherskite, pen poised to paper.

'I'm Gideon Byrd, with a y.'

'Gideon with a y?'

'No, Byrd.'

'And what are you here for?'

'I'm here for protection.'

'And whose protection would that be?'

'That would be Maudelin's (slight pause) and Mildread's.'

Mildread knew he'd only added her name to be polite but since Mr Blatherskite thought that she was Maudelin, she supposed it was all much of a muchness.

'I see,' said Mr Blatherskite, furiously taking notes. 'So you think the girls need protection?'

'Yes.'

'From what, pray tell?'

'Well, from you for a start, but I also think someone might be trying to kill them.'

'And a blood plum winked at us in Wildwood,' added Jet. She was tucked up in the window seat and had already taken two of the teacakes off the tray. She reached over to grab another one, spilling crumbs upon the carpet.

Mysteriously they seemed to be swept up neatly into a small pile and pushed under the tea-table. Even stranger still was the cup of tea in Jet's hand that wobbled and tilted and seemed in danger of spilling but was miraculously caught in mid-air and returned to its saucer by an invisible hand.

'Thank you, Aunt P,' mumbled Jet through a mouthful of crumbs.

Mr Blatherskite looked from the teacup to the children. Gideon studied a corner of the ceiling and the Bellwether twins sat motionless and expressionless on the settee. But, although they didn't say a word, they were not exactly silent.

Should we tell him about the body? Maudelin thought to Mildread.

Why not? Mildread thought to Maudelin. *He might be able to help.*

It looked doubtful but they were willing to give it a go.

'We found a body beneath the blackberry bush,' said Maudelin.

'And we think it's all connected,' added Mildread.

Mr Blatherskite looked sceptical. Actually, he looked constipated, but he didn't believe a word of it either, so after a few more short questions and even shorter answers he declared he had enough information from Gideon and Jet who were now free to leave. They both stayed exactly where they were so Mr Blatherskite spent the rest of the interview ignoring them.

The Bellwether twins were hoping that with all this probing he would reach the same conclusion they had – that the ferry accident (and everything else that had happened to them) was connected to that body beneath the blackberry bush – but it was not to be.

'According to my report, your uncle has quite a long history of accidents at sea.'

The twins exchanged glances. This was going to take a while. They would need more tea. They were just about to offer Mr Blatherskite another refreshing cup when a commotion at the front door stopped everyone and everything in its tracks. Something very loud and quite persistent was intent on breaking through the door. For one silly moment, Mildread thought the sea monster had crawled up the side of the cliff and was throwing itself at their door. She held her breath (well, it had saved her the last time) and Maudelin held hers, too, as someone (or something) burst into the entrance hall.

Danger lurks below the surface

'**D**arlings!' exclaimed Mademoiselle, triumphantly. 'Your father has freed zee pigeon from zee coop!'

All at once the house was filled with noise and excitement.

And footsteps running in all directions.

And Miss Crawford cawing and flapping at the door.

And Uncle Barnaby kicking off his muddy gumboots and shrugging out of his wet raincoat and hanging it on the coat rack in the hallway.

And their father (accidentally mistaken for a coat rack) disentangling himself from Uncle Barnaby's enormous coat and hanging it in the proper place.

And Mademoiselle cooing in French and flinging her arms in every direction.

And Olga, running down the hallway with a plate of teacakes as she tried to give everyone a bite to eat as soon as they stepped through the door (except for Miss Crawford whom she shooed away crossly), tripping over Uncle Barnaby's boots in the process and almost dropping all the cakes onto the floor.

And the ghost of Great Aunt Prunella gliding through everyone's tangled feet with a dustpan and brush.

And Gideon, Jet, Mildread and Maudelin rushing into the hallway and talking to everybody at once.

Whilst Mr Blatherskite, completely horrified by the chaos, hurled himself through the front door and down the path.

And nobody tried to stop him.

When everybody had finally calmed down, Mademoiselle said, 'No need for any of zee fuss or bother.'

'Oh, but this is too exciting for words,' breathed Olga. 'I never thought I'd see the day when someone would have the gall to arrest you, Mademoiselle.'

'It is a simple error of zee judgement.'

'It's a travesty of justice,' snorted Uncle Barnaby.

Olga insisted that everybody convene in the kitchen for what promised to be a splendid afternoon tea but whilst the others stampeded down the hallway, the Bellwether twins held back and helped Mademoiselle out of her coat and hat, the voluminous sleeves of her kaftan getting caught in the bracelets and beads that jingled and jangled noisily.

'Uncle Barnaby said you had a premonition,' said Mildread.

'It's a gift,' she sighed. 'I knew zee instant you were in danger.'

'Why didn't you warn us about the runaway van and the teashop collapsing and the clifftop crumbling into the sea?' asked Maudelin.

'Small potatoes,' sniffed Mademoiselle. 'I only deal with zee big stuff.'

'So did you feel it in your bones?'

'No, it wasn't exactly in my bones.'

'Then a rumbling in your gut?'

'No.'

'Perhaps it was a mystical warning on the wind?'

'Don't be ridiculous, nothing as nonsensical as that.'

'But how did you know we were in danger out there in the middle of the sea?'

'Is it not enough to know that danger lurks below zee surface?'

'So did you think that something hidden beneath the sea would attack us, like a sea serpent?' asked Mildread hopefully.

'Who can say?' said Mademoiselle enigmatically.

But Mildread and Maudelin couldn't help thinking that she could say if she wanted to, but clearly she did not (want to, that is), and that's an entirely different kettle of fish.

Gideon's face had gone the colour of his freckles again as Maudelin recounted their miraculous recovery from the sea. Since no one except Mildread had seen anything fishy beneath the waves, the others assumed that Gideon had done all the saving.

Uncle Barnaby slapped him on the back and said, 'Well done, my boy.'

With everyone seated around the kitchen table, Mildread decided the time had come to solve these mysteries once and for all. She was not so impressed by Gideon's bravery and, if anything, the conversation with Mademoiselle had made her even keener to dig deeper.

'We need to find out what's going on around here,' she said, turning to Gideon, 'beginning with…'

'The body beneath the blackberry bush,' Maudelin chimed in (again).

Mildread scowled at her but said (and thought) nothing.

'Still unidentified,' their father said.

'Well, who could it be?' asked Jet.

They set about making a list:

1. Aunt Prunella. Said to have died in her rocking chair. (The girls couldn't confess that they'd already dug up her body to check!)

2. Aunt Emily. Plunged (or pushed?) off a cliff. Very near to the burial site.

3. Mildread and Maudelin's mother, Elizabeth. Been gone for ages. Sure, she was still sending parcels and postcards, but who's to say they were really from her?

4. Jet's family. Who were they? And, more importantly, WHERE were they?

5. Mrs Dimple's husband. Well, she must have had one. Was Mademoiselle correct in thinking that she put 'poison' in the tea?

6. Gideon's father. No one ever spoke of him but rumour has it he robbed a jewellery store and took it on the lam (that means he's been on the run ever since). Could he have been double-crossed by a crooked partner?

And let's not forget Gideon's mother, Dottie Byrd. Her whereabouts were sketchy at the best of times but just how long had it actually been since anyone had really seen her? Then again, maybe she was the one causing all the trouble. What if all these strange things kept happening whenever Gideon was about because she was trying to keep him away from the Bellwethers? She was batty at the best of times but what if she'd now gone completely round the bend? What if she thought Gideon was becoming too attached to them? Could she be jealous, or simply fearful that he'd end up with the wrong crowd? The

Bellwethers had a long history of being accused of such a thing. Centuries ago their ancestors were chased through the village with burning sticks.

Could Gideon be the cause of all this, thought Mildread.

'No,' hissed Maudelin under her breath as she gave Mildread a deathly stare, 'he could not!'

'He could not what?' asked Gideon, looking thoroughly confused.

But before Maudelin could explain (and, really, what could she say?), the broom in the corner of the room suddenly fell to the floor.

'Company's coming,' said Jet. 'Birdy says it's an old superstition that whenever a broom unexpectedly falls it means company is on the way.'

It's true, she did say that.

'People have been coming in and out of this house all day,' said Olga. 'Who on earth is left?'

Who on earth indeed, for precisely at that moment there came a knock upon the door and events began to take a most unusual turn.

Never speak ill of the dead

A well-heeled woman in her late fifties cautiously entered the room. She seemed a little taken aback by the crowd in the kitchen, not to mention Miss Crawford flapping at the window, but she managed to quickly regain her composure.

'My name is Caroline Pettifogger,' she said. 'My husband, Horatio, is the Mayor of Bitterly Bay.'

'Yes, we know who you are, Caroline,' said Uncle Barnaby, a little impatiently.

Caroline was one of those women who liked to put on airs and graces. Everybody in Bitterly Bay knew everybody else so there was no need for Caroline to be so formal. Unfortunately, that is the way Caroline liked it to be, like it or not.

Olga put the kettle on and passed her a khrustyky pastry.

'I wouldn't normally intrude like this,' said Caroline, sitting down stiffly in a chair and eyeing the pastry with suspicion, 'but I've just had a visit by the most awful man. He interrogated me for the longest of time, implying all sorts of improprieties. He's some sort of…'

'Transport Accident Investigator,' chorused everyone.

'Oh, you've met him?'

'What was he saying?' asked Uncle Barnaby, gruffly.

'Well he thinks my husband may have been involved in the sinking of your boat. Ridiculous really, Horatio has never even got the hem of his trouser-leg wet – he cannot swim, I'm afraid – therefore the idea that he would be tinkering with your boat is positively absurd. We were only on the jetty this morning to officially welcome any prominent visitors to our island. People so rarely come to our little inlet so one must do one's very best to make the right ones feel special when they do dock in our harbour. Don't you think?'

Everybody at the table nodded (including Miss Crawford) but nobody thought anything of the sort (except for Miss Crawford who can be quite a snob at times).

'Did anyone come?' asked Mildread, in the hope that it might throw some light on the body found beneath the blackberry bush.

'No,' replied Caroline, 'at least nobody worth bothering with, but I told that nasty investigator that he ought to be more concerned with that strange woman standing on the clifftop, staring at you,' she said, pointing to Barnaby.

'Me?' gasped Uncle Barnaby. 'A strange woman's been staring at me from the clifftop?'

'Yes,' said Caroline. 'Isn't that what I just said?'

'But who is she?'

'I have no idea,' said Caroline, 'but I told that snippy little snoop that he ought to stop focussing his investigation on you, Maudelin (she said to Mildread), and you, Mildread (she said to Maudelin), and start looking for that woman on the clifftop. I told him to come straight over here and confront the matter head on but that pathetic little weasel kept mumbling something about due diligence and lining all his ducks in a row and who, I ask you, has time for all that when there is the urgent matter of clearing my husband's name? He is the Mayor of this town. He has obligations, and a reputation, and there are certain expectations, and, besides, we have reservations... for dinner on the mainland. So I decided the best thing to do was to put on my hat and coat and see to the matter myself. By the way, these pastries are delicious.'

'Thank you,' said Olga.

'Who is that woman leaning up against the salt shaker?' asked Caroline.

'That's Emily,' said Uncle Barnaby, 'my wife.'

'We think she drowned,' said Jet, through a mouthful of pastry, 'but we're not entirely sure.'

'I'm certain I've seen her somewhere before,' said Caroline. 'In fact, I think she's the strange woman we saw on the clifftop.'

A crack of thunder exploded onto the darkening sky. Everybody jumped. Someone dropped their khrustyky and Miss Crawford eyed it longingly through the window pane. Caroline pointed an accusatory finger at the photograph of Aunt Emily and said, 'She's a stalker.'

You could have heard a pin drop. Miss Crawford cocked her head to one side as if to say w*hat on earth are you talking about?*

And so Caroline explained.

'She was standing on the clifftop, staring out to sea, not moving a single muscle. My husband waved to her, just to be polite. It is part of his job, you understand. But she just kept on staring, straight at your boat. And she had a stick in her hand. Horatio thought it looked like a gun but that's only because she held it strangely, like she was pointing it at someone. But it was knobbly and twisted like a stick, so I don't know. She was creepy, though, and completely fixated on your vessel.'

'What was she doing up there?' asked Barnaby.

Everyone looked at Caroline but she shook her head, as puzzled as the rest of them. 'We turned our attention back to the jetty and when we looked up again, she was gone.'

Could it be…?

Everyone looked at the photo of Emily, then at Barnaby, then back to Emily and a little sob caught in the back of Barnaby's throat.

'If Emily is alive then why hasn't she come home?' he cried.

'It's those eyes,' said Jet, squinting at the photo.

'What are you talking about? She has two, just like the rest of us.'

'If it is Emily, and at this point we don't know that for sure,' said Mildread and Maudelin's father, 'then there must be some reason why she hasn't come home.'

'Amnesia?' suggested Mildread.

'A lousy sense of direction,' said Maudelin.

'A hectic schedule,' said Caroline.

'She hates my cooking,' said Olga.

'She thinks everyone else is dead,' said Mademoiselle.

'She no longer loves me,' Barnaby sighed. 'Maybe that's why she was staring at my boat. Maybe she did something to it because she wants me dead.'

'Or maybe she thinks you're dead, too, and doesn't want anyone else using your boat,' said Gideon.

'That makes sense,' said Jet. 'You were lost at sea for many years. Maybe she jumped off the cliff because she thought you were dead.'

'But you weren't,' said Mildread.

'And maybe she isn't, either,' said Maudelin.

Miss Crawford pecked at the glass and gave Mademoiselle a beady stare. Did she know the truth of things like only a wise crow could? Perhaps Mademoiselle's premonitions and prognostications were not simply wild stabs in the dark.

'We need to inform the police,' said Caroline, 'and we haven't a moment to lose.'

Try not to panic

Constables Ray and Jay had just made a cup of tea and were selecting their dunking biscuits when the crowd burst through the door and surged forth.

Miss Crawford, cawing and flapping, hopped across the countertop before settling on a pile of paperwork. More crows gathered outside as the sky blackened.

Constable Ray dropped his biscuit in his tea and scowled. 'What's all this about?'

'Murder,' said Mildread.

'And mayhem,' said Maudelin.

'I see,' said Constable Ray.

'Glad we cleared that up,' said Constable Jay. 'Does this mean you've identified the body beneath the blackberry bush?'

Mildread and Maudelin's father shook his head. 'Not yet,' he said, 'but I think we're getting closer.'

'There's been a possible sighting of my Emily,' said Uncle Barnaby.

'You don't say,' said Constable Ray, fishing about in his tea for his soggy biscuit.

'I do say,' said Barnaby.

'Oh you do, do you?' said Constable Jay. 'Do tell.'

He was a little cross that Uncle Barnaby's boat had led them on a wild goose chase. Forensics had just sent in a report saying that whilst they could categorically confirm that Barnaby's boat *was* a bomb (in other words, a complete wreck) they must regretfully advise that no bomb was found *on* the boat. Were Barnaby to discover his beloved boat described in that way, he would probably have a fit. Constable Jay quite sensibly hid the offending paperwork under his cup.

'Are you trying to tell us,' he continued, 'that Emily Bellwether sank your boat?'

'No,' said Uncle Barnaby hotly, 'she would never do such a thing.'

'We're not here to talk about the boat,' said Maudelin.

'Well, if you're not here to talk about the body or the boat, then what else is there?'

Mildread opened her mouth. Was this the perfect time to tell everyone that something rather magnificent was lurking at the bottom of the sea?

Jet also opened her mouth. Should she mention the witches in the wood?

Gideon took a step back. No need to drag his dangerously unstable mother into the mix. There was quite enough going on as it was.

But Caroline Pettifogger seized the moment – after all she was entitled to – and took a decisive step forward. 'I saw this woman staring at Barnaby Bellwether's boat shortly before it sank,' she said, thrusting forward the photograph of Emily that she'd swiped from the salt shaker. 'I'm not saying she sank the boat for certain but my husband, Horatio, the Mayor of this fine town, thought he spotted a gun in her hand and I must confess her stare was icy cold and cannot be ignored.'

'I see,' said Constable Ray, wishing he could ignore the lot of them. 'Serious charges there, I think, very serious indeed.'

'I don't care if she sank my boat,' Barnaby sighed. 'I just want to know if she's alive.'

The truth was Barnaby hadn't wanted to come to the station at all. He'd wanted to mount a search party at once but dusk was falling and a storm was brewing and the others had finally convinced him that things needed to be done properly in order to get the best results.

He'd also wanted to stay back at the house in case Emily suddenly turned up but the likelihood of that happening was really rather slim and, besides, they assured him, Aunt Prunella would still be there to welcome her home if need be.

Gideon had been about to say that he didn't believe in ghosts when he'd caught sight of a tiny flutter in the corner of his eye as they were piling into the hearse and when he'd looked up he could've sworn he'd seen someone waving at him from the attic window.

He'd done a half-wave back, just to be polite.

Constables Ray and Jay, however, insisted on doing everything by the book, which involved a lot of paperwork and questioning and going over statements at least a dozen times and everyone was getting rather weary of it all when suddenly the door flung open again and Mr Blatherskite marched in.

'How dare you carry on this investigation without me,' he spluttered.

'Just what we need,' sighed Constable Ray, 'another joker.'

'I can assure you, I don't find any of this remotely amusing,' huffed Mr Blatherskite. 'Don't try and pull the wool over my eyes. I saw your hearse careening down the hilltop and hurtling through town.'

'I hope you were wearing seatbelts,' said Constable Jay.

'Do you really think you can carry on this investigation without me? Don't you know that I'm a...'

'Transport Accident Investigator,' shouted everyone. 'We know!'

Mr Blatherskite thumped his thick folder onto the counter. 'I deserve to know what's going on,' he said.

'I'd like to know, too,' said Constable Ray.

'That goes without saying,' said Constable Jay.

Uncle Barnaby wanted to issue an All-Points Bulletin (known as an APB), alerting everyone to be on the lookout for his wife but the constables pointed to a faded Missing Person poster on the bulletin board.

'But we have a fresh sighting,' argued Uncle Barnaby.

'That is not a strong enough reason to issue new posters,' said Constable Ray. 'We don't even know for certain that the person spotted on the clifftop is your missing wife. Why would she be standing on the clifftop, staring out to sea? Why not go home instead?'

'Because she thinks I'm dead,' wailed Uncle Barnaby.

'Some people do not have zee gift of second sight,' said Mademoiselle.

'We do not know for certain if this woman, whoever she is, is responsible for plunging your boat into the sea,' sniffed Mr Blatherskite. 'It could have been a faulty valve in the engine. It could have been a leaky hull. It could have been anything (and at this point he glared at the Bellwether twins) but until I finish my investigation there will be no official ruling on the case.'

'I think it was a bomb,' said Gideon, but only because he liked to think that everything was.

'We know it wasn't a bomb,' said Constable Jay, retrieving the tea-stained forensic report from underneath his cup. 'But it could have been a strange woman with a gun shooting out the engine,' he conceded. 'All the same, that still doesn't mean it was Emily Bellwether.'

Could it be just one person doing all these bad things around town – burying bodies, driving like a lunatic, blowing up teashops and clifftops and sinking boats – or were they dealing with a group of people, either working together or independent of each other?

'All of these events could be entirely unrelated,' said Constable Jay.

'And entirely accidental,' added Mr Blatherskite with a sniff.

(He really ought to do something about that cold of his.)

'And no arrests shall be made until all of these possibilities have been thoroughly explored,' said Constable Ray, 'so I suggest everyone goes home and tries not to panic.'

'It's a bit too late for that,' said Caroline but all the same, she allowed herself to be shepherded out the door with everyone else and, reluctantly, the crowd dispersed and everybody headed for home.

'And let that be the end of it,' said Constable Ray.

But, of course, it wasn't.

In many forms shall the dead return

'There's something not quite right about all this,' said Mildread.

'I've been thinking the same thing,' said Maudelin.

'Well of course you have.'

They left Gideon and Jet at the edge of Wildwood (arguing about whether they should go in or not) and followed their father down to the basement. They were eager to see what sort of progress had been made on that mysterious body that someone had seen fit to bury beneath the blackberry bush.

'Do you think the blackberries are a clue?' asked Maudelin.

'I wouldn't think so,' said Mildread. 'What does it matter where you're buried?'

I know I said it doesn't matter a jot to the one who is dead but, for the record, it can matter greatly to the ones who are left behind.

'Well, whoever it was, they didn't just drop dead whilst picking blackberries.'

'That's probably unlikely,' agreed their father.

'So why were they buried there? Was someone trying to cover their tracks?'

You have to admit, a prickly blackberry bush is the ideal spot if you don't want someone poking about.

'Are there any clues to be found on the body?' asked Mildread.

'I'm not at liberty to say,' their father said.

'Why not? Is it someone we know?'

Mildread and Maudelin peered down at the rotting corpse and tried to picture Aunt Emily, but they had no real memories of their aunt, only that photograph propped up against the salt shaker. They considered propping the corpse up into a sitting position but their father, no doubt anticipating their plans, told them not to touch the body.

'It's still under investigation,' he said.

Out of respect for the dead (and the serious task of autopsy), Mildread and Maudelin kept their impulses in check.

'Let's use our eyes to gather as much information as we can,' said Mildread. 'Then we'll tell Jet.'

'And Gid,' added Maudelin.

'Yes, him too.'

They could see a few tufts of hair sticking to the skull and one of the eyes was still attached to the optic nerve, dangling on the cheek. Mildread and Maudelin leant in close to the rotting flesh and breathed in the heady stench of decay.

'Have you noticed that every time we discuss this body something catastrophic happens?' said Mildread.

'Nothing's happening now,' said Maudelin.

'Now is our chance to sneak off into Wildwood and find out what we're dealing with,' said Jet.

'But it's getting dark,' said Gideon.

'So grab a lantern.'

Jet ignored the broken fishing rod leaning against the hedgerow and the pile of old books scattered across the lawn, their spines punctured by ragged holes.

She ignored the crows sitting in the plum tree. One or two cawed softly at her approach.

But nothing was going to distract her this time. She was determined to breach the invisible line that she was sure the witches had drawn between her and Wildwood.

She climbed over the stile into the wood, jumped down onto the forest floor, and snatched up the plum, giving it an enormous bite. The juices slid down her face and trickled through her fingers like blood oozing from an open wound.

'And that's how you do it,' she said, munching on her prize and forgetting momentarily that a witch might have done something fiendish to it.

The black crows, their feathers clearly ruffled, flew up into the sky and headed back to Crow Cottage.

Gideon looked around nervously, peering first into the dark wood and then turning and looking back at the Bellwether house, which looked even more sinister in the lengthening shadows of twilight. The full moon cast a ghostly pall over everything.

'Aren't you coming?' said Jet.

'Yes, yes, I'm coming,' said Gideon but his feet refused to move.

He hung back a little, glancing over his shoulder, chewing his bottom lip, and generally emitting a disagreeable mood into the cold night air. He gave an involuntary shudder.

What was he doing here? He hadn't wanted to do this in the first place but he didn't want anyone to think he was chicken. He was beginning to wonder why he hadn't just gone home. He couldn't remember the last time he'd spoken to his mother. She was desperate and panicky at the best of times but she must be worried sick by now. Come to think of it, he was beginning to sound a little desperate and panicky himself.

'We're just going in for a peek,' said Jet, impatiently.

'Famous last words,' Gideon muttered.

Who knows how long Gideon would have flip-flopped back and forth on that stile were it not for the purple plum disappearing, once again, in the blink of an eye. Unfortunately, it was still in Jet's hand and so she disappeared with it.

Gideon stood on the stile and stared in disbelief at the empty clearing.

And then he turned on his heels and ran for the Bellwether house.

The door to the basement was nearly thrown off its hinges as Gideon came thundering down the stairs, crying out in a panic, 'She's gone, she's gone!'

And Mildread and Maudelin knew exactly who he meant.

Beware the wolf in dead sheep's clothing

Something was crouching down in the darkness on its haunches, its knobbly knuckles trailing in the dead leaves. It tilted its head to one side as if studying its prey carefully, then inched slowly across the ground before straightening up and stretching out a mud-caked hand. It moved slowly, as if trying not to frighten her. And then a huge, dark shadow swooped down and suddenly the creature grabbed Jet's wrist and hissed, 'Run!'

She ran. She had no choice. The creature's dirty fingers were wrapped tightly around her wrist. She tripped over twisting tree roots and swatted aside the branches scratching at her skin. And all the while the creature kept a firm grip on her wrist, nearly wrenching the arm from its socket. An ear-splitting shriek and the heavy sound of beating wings followed them deep into Wildwood.

With lungs burning, ears ringing, legs aching, eyes watering, heart pounding, skin tingling, nose running, neck sweating and breath coming out all ragged and raw, Jet ran.

I'm sure if you heard her coming, you would be forgiven for thinking a giant rhinoceros was crashing through the undergrowth.

The creature slowed down and then shimmied effortlessly through a tiny gap between the thick branches. Jet hesitated. Surely it didn't expect her to follow it in there?

It did.

Somehow it wrenched her through, even though it involved a lot of tugging and twisting. At one point it even sat on her head, trying to squash it through a hole that looked about the size of an eyeball. Speaking of eyeballs, it felt like Jet's were about to pop right out of her head. But still she ran.

It was hard to distinguish shadow from shrub through the twilight as the leaves and branches swallowed up their trail so she concentrated on running and avoiding a stick in the eye. At one point she tripped and ended up with a mouthful of dirt but the creature dragged her to her feet and said, 'No time to stop and snack on bugs and dirt, we still have a way to go.'

'What was that big, dark thing that swooped down on us?' panted Jet. 'Ooh, I think I've got a stitch. Do you know what it was? Was it a witch? I bet it was a witch. It looked like a witch to me. Do you think it was a witch?'

'I suppose so,' said the creature. It had no idea what a witch was.

Jet stopped to catch her breath and look about. 'I think it's a witch that can shapeshift into a gigantic bird of prey so that it can peck out our eyes and swallow our hearts whole.'

'How about we wait until it catches us, just to be sure?' said the creature. 'Only I can't think why else you're standing here, rooted to the spot, when I clearly told you to run.'

'I ran,' protested Jet.

'Well, I didn't tell you to stop.'

'I'm waiting for Gideon to catch up.'

Jet felt a little guilty that up until now she hadn't really given him a second thought.

'What is a Gideon?'

'That's his name. Gideon Byrd.'

The creature looked up at the sky as if expecting him to swoop down upon them.

'He's not an actual bird. It's just his name. He's supposed to be behind us,' said Jet, pointing to the gap in the trees from which they'd just emerged, which was now only about the size of an eyeball, as expected. 'Oh, forget it,' said Jet. 'He won't bother following us now. Where are we going?'

'Away,' said the creature. Then before Jet could annoy it further, it added, 'Away from the bird-witch. She's been watching you. I've seen her'

'You have? But why would she be watching me?'

'Because you found one of her dead bodies.'

'One of them? You mean there's more than one?'

The creature nodded. 'There are lots of them. Come on, I'll show you.' And it was on the move again.

Jet wasn't sure if it was such a good idea to follow a strange, dirty creature deep into Wildwood where lots of bodies were buried. She hadn't actually seen a witch and so she only had the creature's word that a witch was watching them.

'Do you have a name?' she asked. For some ridiculous reason she thought this might make it seem less frightening.

'Everybody has a name,' it said.

'Well, what is it?'

'Pete Moss.'

'I'm Jet, in case you're interested.'

It wasn't.

'So what are you – goblin, pixie, or some other woodland creature?'

She had been trying to get a good look at it as they ran and at first she'd thought it was incredibly hairy before realising it was wearing a fur pelt across its shoulders – a filthy, matted, stinky piece of fur that had passed dead a very long time ago. There was bound to be a colony of germs plotting to overthrow the host at any moment.

'I'm a boy,' he said, turning to face her.

'Really? You look very skinny for a boy.'

'I'm a skinny boy, what of it?'

'And you have big ears.'

'Do I?' Pete grabbed his ears and pulled at them.

Jet was about to laugh when she was struck by a sudden thought. What if it was only a bird that had followed them into Wildwood? And what if the real danger was this strange boy? He hadn't even needed to lure her into his trap, she'd come willingly. And now here they were, deep in the forbidden wood, with no one else around to hear her scream. And Pete Moss, the skinny, big-eared boy, was baring his black teeth and looking for all the world like a wolf in dead sheep's clothing.

'Goodness, Pete,' said Jet. 'What big teeth you have.'

Do not go gentle into that good night

'She's gone, she's gone!'

And Mildread and Maudelin knew exactly who Gideon meant.

They ran up the basement stairs as fast as they could, their father right behind them. As he ran, he shouted out to the others, 'Barnaby, get the gun! Olga, fetch the lanterns! Mademoiselle! Mademoiselle!'

He didn't need to call out to her, for Mademoiselle was already at the back door, her shawl wrapped tightly against the cold chill of the night air.

'Blast and bother!' shouted Barnaby, struggling into his boots and overcoat.

'Why do adults have to make such a song and dance about everything?' puffed Gideon, quite forgetting that he was responsible for all the panic.

They leapt over the low stone wall and raced to the stile but the sky immediately filled with crows, their beating wings driving the Bellwethers back into the nearby graveyard. Uncle Barnaby blustered and raised his blunderbuss (a very big gun) but the crows snatched it out of his hands with their sharp claws and began to caw so loudly and so terribly that everyone was forced to cover their ears and run.

Gideon, however, quickly discovered that no matter how fast he pumped his legs, he ended up moving further away from the others...

And higher up.

Maudelin watched in horror as the crows grabbed hold of Gideon and snatched him away.

Without thinking, she ran after him and, as I have said a hundred times before, where one goes the other follows. It felt very strange to Mildread to not take the lead this time and to find herself following in Maudelin's panicked footsteps, but she had no hesitation. It no longer mattered whether Gideon was friend or foe. If Maudelin was prepared to go to the ends of the earth for him, then Mildread would go there, too.

She grabbed a lantern out of Olga's trembling hand as she sprinted by.

Their father called after them. 'Girls, come back!'

'It's too late,' said Mademoiselle, 'zee time has come for zee truth to be told.'

The truth?

That feeling of dread trickled down Mildread's spine but instead of leaning into it (which I will admit is a little difficult to do when you're running), somewhere at the very back of her mind a distant memory was dredged up from a dark corner.

It was of that clawed hand poking out of the soil.

She had assumed that it was rigor mortis. Dead bodies shrink and contract as they decay. Dead flesh invariably wastes away. But this hand had looked slightly different.

She thought back in her mind to that wonderfully miserable moment when she'd first spied those skeletal fingers. She remembered Maudelin sitting in the graveyard with a book in her hand and a spider sprawling across the page, its long legs mimicking the skeletal bones of a hand.

There was something about that book in her hand, something familiar about Maudelin's hand, and the spider's long legs, that connected them to that clawed hand in the dirt.

They were the same, thought Mildread; the same spidery curling of the fingers. And that's when she realised that the hand poking out of the dirt must have been holding a book.

But what book and where was it now?

She wanted to tell Maudelin of her suspicions but Maudelin had more important things on her mind for the crows had carried Gideon up to the top of the broken lighthouse and there was nothing for it but to follow.

The broken lighthouse was a very dangerous place to be so naturally it appealed to Mildread and Maudelin. There were one hundred and sixty-seven steps to the top. The view was to die for, especially if you leant against the rotten iron railing and it crumbled beneath your fingertips but, considering the trickiness of the steps, the climb alone could kill you.

As if that would stop Mildread and Maudelin.

They tripped up the troublesome stairs and poked their heads up through the trapdoor and into the beacon room, pushing the lantern forward. And there, sitting on the cold concrete floor, trussed up like a turkey, was Gideon, the lantern at his feet throwing a dull glow around the walls. Behind him lay shattered glass from one of the panes. The crows had smashed their way into the lighthouse and several of them now sat on the railing outside. The wind howled through the exposed pane and whipped around the beacon. Raindrops hurtled into the room almost horizontal. Gideon had a gag across his mouth but his eyes opened wide when he saw Maudelin and she quickly rushed to his side.

'Oh Gid,' she sobbed, 'I thought you were dead.' She flung her arms around his neck and squeezed tight.

Gideon gave a little squawk and his freckles turned pink until Mildread managed to calm Maudelin down and get her to stop choking him. Mildread removed the gag and began to untie the ropes around his wrist.

'Birdy Black,' gasped Gideon.

'Oh no, has the witch got her too?'

'She *is* the witch!'

And right at that moment, Birdy stepped out of the shadows and kicked the trapdoor shut.

Rage against the dying of the light

If you've ever been the victim of a nasty shock, you will know that it takes your brain several seconds to register what your eyes are trying to tell it. It's called disbelief and it can cloud even the smartest minds from seeing the obvious. Birdy Black was supposed to be Jet's protector. She had taken her in and cared for her and warned her many times of the dangers that lurked in Wildwood. Therefore, she could not possibly be a witch. It just couldn't be true.

And so, you see, as Mildread and Maudelin spun around to face her in the broken lighthouse, Birdy had the upper hand. She had time to grab a thick rope and wind it around Mildread and Gideon and Maudelin before anyone had a chance to stop her. The rope pinned their arms to their sides and they were rendered helpless. Birdy pushed them to the ground and tied their feet together and now all three of them were trussed up like turkeys.

I'm not sure what Jet would have made of this. Would she have been horrified at the thought that her beloved protector could have hidden such a tremendous secret from her or would she have shouted in delight at the wonderful news that a witch had been hiding from her in plain sight?

At any rate, she probably would not have bothered going on a wild goose chase with that skinny, big-eared boy. Then again, if she hadn't followed him deep into Wildwood, then she might never have learnt the awful truth that Birdy had obviously been trying to keep from her.

I mean, think about it; sinister foreboding and malicious intent? What did that mean, anyway?

Obviously Birdy had filled their minds with silly superstition to prevent them from digging deeper. One can only imagine what danger Jet was now in, without even realising it.

She stood in a clearing under the pale moonlight. The trees were ghostly grey shadows as the milky white fog gently wrapped itself around them.

That ever-present fog! Jet was certain it hid many secrets and prevented anyone, especially herself, from seeing things clearly.

'Where are we?' she complained. 'What's beyond all this fog?'

She strained her eyes and tried to pick apart the lumpy shapes that loomed before her. Where was Mrs Fossle when you needed her?

She could hear water and her skin felt damp so they must be near the sea.

'Are we standing at the edge of a cliff?' she demanded to know. 'Don't get any ideas about pushing me off.'

'It's not the sea, it's just a river,' said Pete. 'It's right at your feet. A girl drowned in it, so it's a little tricky to cross.'

Jet felt a shiver run down her spine. According to old superstition, that means someone is walking over your grave. Believe me, I know how it feels. They do it to me all the time. One minute I'm happily gazing up at the grey clouds swirling over my head, the water rippling gently across my face, and the next minute there's a foot on my cheek, grinding my bones into the sharp rocks with tiny pebbles embedding themselves into places where you would not want a pebble to go.

And do I hear a whisper of apology?

No, I do not.

Not so much as a by-your-leave.

But I digress.

Jet, when she felt that shiver, instantly wondered whose grave was being trampled upon for she knew it could not be hers.

'Do you know who it was that was buried under the blackberry bush?' she asked. 'Do you know how they died?'

'No, but the crow might know,' said Pete.

'The crow? Do you mean Miss Crawford?'

'I don't know what her name is. You called her a witch before but sometimes she's a crow. She has a very sharp beak and beady black eyes and a feathery cape on her back. And she comes from over there.'

He pointed into the distance to the curling mist beyond the river.

'She creeps up to the edge of the wood every time a body is found and picks at its bones.'

Jet felt the hair on the back of her neck prickle. She squinted into the mist. 'What's in there?' She couldn't help it. Her fearless curiosity made her want to know.

'Nothing,' said Pete, 'just swirling fog.'

'But it must lead to somewhere,' said Jet. 'Is it the edge of the cliff? Can you hear the waves crashing below?'

'It's just a wet and heavy silence,' said Pete. 'And it feels empty and lonely. I don't like it so I don't go in there anymore. The crow-witch tried to make me follow her out of the woods but I won't go. I don't want her to pick at my bones, too.'

'Why would she pick your bones?'

'Because that's what crows do.'

'So you've been hiding in here all this time? Where is your family?'

'I think they're buried on the other side of the river. There are lots of gravestones over there with funny names. I don't know what my family was called. I left them when I was very young, or they left me, I'm not sure which.'

'But how did you survive in Wildwood all on your own?' asked Jet. She was mightily impressed but also terribly confused. She wanted to cross the river and read the gravestones but already the mist was pulling at her ankles and wrists.

'You have to close your eyes,' said Pete. 'The fog will let you go if you close your eyes. Follow the sound of the water. You can step on the rocks to cross safely but you have to keep your eyes shut. The girl who drowned still lies at the bottom, under the water, and if she catches your eye, you're done for.'

(You grab one person's ankles as a joke, and you are forever marked as a troublemaker.)

'But if she drowned, then how can she do any harm?'

Pete shrugged. 'She must be one of those witches that you like so much.'

'A witch?' Jet perked right up at the thought of being so close to a witch but then she hesitated. Was it such a good idea to be within grabbing distance of one?

'Don't worry,' said Pete, 'I've had lots of practice, so I can safely cross over. Take my hand and I'll lead you there. But don't look down.'

Jet looked at Pete and tried to detect any signs of subterfuge. Could this be a trick to get her to trust him so that he could drown her in the river? Well, he'd be in for a rude shock if that was his plan. He'd discover quick smart that Jet was (literally) no push-over. And so she closed her eyes and allowed him to lead her over the river. She felt the wispy tendrils of the mist release their grip on her but she still felt the coldness deep inside her bones.

Way, way at the back of her mind a little voice was trying to warn her. But (as usual) Jet ignored it.

I watched from my watery vantage point but made no move to stop them.

'One more step,' said Pete, 'and then you're on the other side.'

Jet took a step and opened her eyes. All around her were the scattered headstones of many graves. There were no flowers resting on the dirt. It was just an isolated, desolate graveyard and it gave her the creeps, big time. Jet steadied her nerves and peered down at the nearest gravestone.

Instantly, she heard the sound of beating wings and the sharp call of the crows, and it took a frantic moment to realise that the bone-chilling scream erupting into the cold night air belonged to her.

Let there be light

Jet could feel her body moving up and away from the graves and at first she felt relief before realising that she was actually being lifted up into the air by the crows. Their talons were digging into her shoulders, their heavy, beating wings sounding loud in her ears. She felt their immense power and it frightened her. But then she looked down and a feeling of joy wiped away the fear. She was weightless and free. She closed her eyes and felt the wind singing around her. She wriggled her toes and imagined that the crow's wings belonged to her and that she, alone, was flying high above Bitterly Bay.

She opened her eyes, hoping to see what lay beyond Wildwood, but the only thing visible was the thick, creamy fog. She couldn't even see Wildwood anymore. What she did see, however, was the broken lighthouse. It loomed before her, menacing and cold, cracked and dark, and with one window shattered, revealing a huge hole like the mouth of a ravenous monster. And she was getting closer to it.

Closer and closer.

Mildread, Maudelin and Gideon were momentarily stunned as the crows burst through the shattered window and deposited Jet onto the lighthouse floor.

'Run!' shouted Gideon, the first to find his voice.

Then, after a slight pause, 'It's Birdy!' shouted Mildread, which was a little confusing for they were now surrounded by birds.

'She's a witch!' shouted Maudelin, which didn't help matters at all, for Jet could not move.

First, she was trying to come to grips with what had just happened to her. People, as a general rule, don't find themselves flying through the air like that and it can take a bit of time to recover from such an event. Secondly, she'd just been dumped, rather unceremoniously, onto a hard, concrete floor. And thirdly, her brain was having a little difficulty trying to work out what her eyes were seeing. Why were her friends tied up on the floor of the broken lighthouse? Why had the crows brought her here? What was Birdy doing with that rope? And why did she have such a strange look on her face, so dark and determined and grim?

'She's a what?' said Jet, rubbing her bruised derriere.

'Not a what, a witch!' (Confusing, right?)

Finally Jet's brain caught up and, as Birdy bent down to get another rope, she stumbled to her feet and ran.

Unfortunately, there weren't a lot of places to go. Just round and round the beacon pedestal or out onto the rickety balcony that circled the top of the lighthouse. Jet stepped back through the broken window. The wind attacked her face and it felt like tiny knives were stabbing at her cheeks. She pressed her back against the large windows and inched herself along, praying that the steel girders beneath her feet would not fall away and pitch her into the sea. She could hear the waves crashing angrily against the rocks but it was too dark to see anything.

The lantern on the floor was not doing such a great job of illuminating the lighthouse, either. The pedestal in the middle of the room upon which the beacon stood cast all sorts of odd shapes across the walls and Birdy's features were being distorted by shadow so that she appeared both old and frail and fearsome and strong in turn. As if transforming from a disguise to one's true self.

Birdy stepped onto the balcony, barring Jet's way back in. She straightened her back and uncoiled the bun at the base of her neck, loosening her grey tendrils. White powder fell to the ground revealing a glossy black mane. She no longer looked old and frail. She cackled, just like a wicked witch would do, or it could have been a hacking cough caused by all the talcum powder shaken from her hair but either way Jet felt a shiver run all the way down her spine.

'Why are you doing this?' she cried. 'And why would you make yourself look older than you really are, who on earth does that?'

'It's complicated,' said Birdy. 'All you need to know is that I am here to facilitate your death.'

'Well, if it's all the same with you, I'm not ready to die just yet.'

'That is unfortunate because nobody can avoid death. Eventually we all end up six feet under.'

(Or in an even shallower grave, if you're that body buried beneath the blackberry bush.)

'I've seen the graves in the woods,' said Jet. 'I know why you wouldn't let us go in there. You didn't want us to see all the bodies you've buried.'

'Oh, that's awful,' said Mildread. I'm not sure what angered her more. That bodies should be in the ground without a proper burial or that she had not had the opportunity to study them in detail first.

'It gets worse,' said Jet. 'Just before the crows snatched me away, I found a gravestone with *my* name on it. Sorry to scupper your plans, Birdy, but I plan to go kicking and screaming to my grave.'

'I would not expect it any other way,' smiled Birdy.

As Jet inched along the unstable balcony, Mildread and Maudelin quietly put their heads together. Since Gideon was wedged in between them, he was reluctantly drawn into their whispered conversation.

'Do you think Birdy buried the body in the blackberry bush?' asked Maudelin.

'I wonder how many others she's killed,' said Mildread.

'Will you two stop thinking about death for just a minute,' said Gideon, crossly. 'We have to figure out how to get out of this alive and save Jet.'

'And how do you propose we do that?' demanded Mildread. 'We're trussed up like turkeys, in case you haven't noticed.'

'If only we could move that lantern,' said Gideon. 'If we could place it on the pedestal then the light would be refracted by all the mirrors surrounding it and it would shine a brilliant light out the windows and blind her.'

Mildread and Maudelin looked at each another. If they could link hands then they could probably move that lantern with their minds. But their arms were strapped to their sides. And Gideon was between them.

'I've got an idea,' whispered Maudelin. 'If I hold onto Gideon's hand and you do the same on your side then maybe our telekinetic energies will surge through his body and connect.'

Maudelin grabbed Gideon's hand and Mildread grabbed the other and they squeezed their eyes shut tight and concentrated just as hard as they could. Gideon felt a tingle in his chest and his freckles felt like they were on fire. The blood in his veins throbbed and his brain buzzed. *This must be how that monster felt when Doctor Frankenstein pulled the switch*, he thought to himself.

He wondered if it always felt this way when you held a girl's hand.

The lantern rose shakily into the air and slowly moved across the room.

Birdy was so intent on reaching Jet that she didn't notice a thing until the lantern finally slotted into place and the mirrors grabbed hold of the light and shone it out to sea.

Jet was flat against the window, her back pressed up to the glass, so the light shone all around her like a magnificent halo but she didn't get it square in the eyes. Not like Birdy. She copped it full on and was instantly blinded. She staggered back and reached out for the railing and, as predicted, it crumbled beneath her fingertips and she was thrown over the balcony and down to the jagged rocks below.

Mildread and Maudelin and Gideon cheered and shouted for Jet to come back inside and she carefully inched her way back into the beacon room.

'Wow,' she said, 'who turned on the light?'

There is more than one way to skin a cat

D o you recall me telling you that the lighthouse could be seen from the centre of town? Well, it seemed like half the townsfolk were roused from their sleep by a brilliant light shining in their faces and so they leapt out of bed in alarm, grabbed their dressing gown and slippers, and high-tailed it up the hill.

'What in blazes is going on?' blustered Barnaby.

There was much too much confusion for his liking. First he'd been told to grab his gun, then it had been snatched away by murderous crows, then Mademoiselle had told him to let the matter rest and now he was being jostled about by townsfolk in their pyjamas.

Mildread, Maudelin, Gideon and Jet emerged from the lighthouse and everyone got terribly excited and began to talk at once and several times the story was told until everyone finally heard it.

Mrs Dimple wheeled her portable urn up the hill and dispatched soothing cups of tea. Mademoiselle brought along a bag of sugar from the pantry. Olga brought cinder toffee – a crunchy sweet named after the cinders in the bottom of the fire, made with caster sugar and black treacle – and everyone enjoyed the full moon feast.

Mr and Mrs Fossle rushed over to their grandson, Gideon, to ensure that he was unharmed.

'Now, now, Louisa, don't fuss over the boy,' said Mr Fossle as Mrs Fossle checked for any visible signs of injury.

'Is the witch dead?' asked Jet as Constables Ray and Jay climbed over the rocks in search of Birdy's broken and battered body.

'We can't find her,' said Constable Ray.

'We need more light,' said Constable Jay.

Everybody leant over the clifftop and shone their lanterns down onto the rocks but it made no difference. No one could see Birdy Black. She wasn't there.

'Perhaps she drowned,' suggested Uncle Barnaby.

'I think she fell straight down,' said Jet, a little uncertainly. 'She should have landed on the rocks and broken her neck.'

But the only thing down there was Constable Ray, Constable Jay, and...

Wait a minute, what's that?

Several people swung their lanterns over the edge of the rocks where a dark shadow moved.

'It's a black crow,' said Mrs Dimple, peering out from between two elbows.

They all watched as the bird took a few unsteady hops across the rocks then tilted her head in that tell-tale way.

'Why, that's Miss Crawford,' said Olga, holding out a cinder toffee. 'What's she doing down there?'

'Maybe she's found the body and is picking at the carcass,' said Jet, remembering what Pete had told her about the crows.

But right at that moment, Miss Crawford flew straight up to the crowd on the clifftop, grabbed the toffee along the way (waste not want not), and disappeared into the inky sky where her sister crows were waiting and before anyone could move, a terrifying sound filled the air all around them.

A huge shape swooped down from the skies and over the trees, heading for the patch of ground in front of the broken lighthouse. It skimmed the turrets and spires (and a gargoyle or two) on the Bellwether house, all the while making a deep guttural growl that sounded like the bellows of a dragon's breath.

Everyone looked up because that's the first thing you do when you think a dragon is hovering over your head. Now you and I both know that it couldn't possibly be a dragon because we know that such things belong in fairy tales and this is not a fairy tale (not even close) but Jet believed in strange and spooky things (such as witches in the woods and ghosts in the attic) and anyone who believed in ghosts and witches probably believed in dragons, too. So, at the very least, we can expect Jet to have been expecting a dragon to breathe its hellfire all over her head. Judging by Gideon's startled, bug-eyed expression and the looks on Mildread and Maudelin's faces, I would say they were expecting something as outrageous as a fire-breathing dragon, too.

But regardless of what was expected, I can definitely say for certain that not one person on the top of that hill at the edge of that clifftop was expecting to see what they actually did see bellowing and bouncing towards them.

It was a hot air balloon.

It landed with a shuddering thud and tipped over to the side and four rather frazzled figures tumbled out. The first one was a bald, bushy-bearded giant. The second was a solid man in top hat and tails. The third was a tall, skinny man with a thin moustache and a silk-lined cape. But it was the fourth occupant who garnered all the attention. She was a girl wearing a black leotard with belt-buckle straps, puffy tulle sleeves, a metal and leather harness, a black tattered and torn tutu with a studded belt wound several times around her waist and black and white striped tights. The only bit of colour in this severe black and white costume was her hair. It was candy-floss pink. And as she tumbled out of the wicker basket, she kicked her legs into the air and cartwheeled onto her feet.

No one quite knew why, but everyone was compelled to clap.

The acrobat smiled but it was a sad smile.

The giant helped the man in top hat and tails out of the fallen basket and with a flourish the man removed his hat and said, 'Ladies and Gentlemen,' in a deep, commanding voice that wavered a little as he spoke. He was all razzle dazzle but clearly he was not completely in command of the situation.

'Ringo?' said a voice from the back of the crowd. As everyone parted to let her through, Mademoiselle cautiously stepped forward.

'Mademoiselle Gabrielle?' The man looked a little uncertain at first and recognition did little to ease his confusion. 'Is that you?'

'Oui,' said Mademoiselle (that's French for yes).

'But the last time I saw you, it was in Paris. What are you doing here? I thought you were dead.'

'That is true,' said Mademoiselle, 'but Elizabeth Bellwether asked me to find her daughters and care for them until she could be reunited with them. I am afraid it has been a very long time. I have almost forgotten zee bright lights and zee sparkle of my beloved Paree (that's how she says Paris).'

'But we have not forgotten you,' said the man in the hat whom Mademoiselle had called Ringo.

His name was Mr Razzmatazz and he was a circus ringmaster so everyone called him Ringo. The others in the balloon basket were also circus performers. There was Gregor the Strongman, Marvello the Magician and Lucinda Creek, the acrobat. They all bowed magnificently before the townsfolk but none of them looked particularly pleased to be there.

'What are you doing in our neck of zee woods?' asked Mademoiselle.

And Ringo answered, 'It was quite by accident, my dear. We were part of a travelling troupe bound for far and exotic places when our balloon fell afoul of a tremendous thunderstorm. I am afraid we were thrown off course and have thus ended up here.'

'It's a miracle you survived,' said Mrs Dimple, offering a restorative cup of tea to the troupe.

'Yes,' said Ringo, looking uncertainly at Mademoiselle. 'We believed we were doomed but clearly the stars have other plans for us.'

'Well, no mind,' said Mademoiselle cheerfully. 'You are here now and that is all that matters.'

But it wasn't all that mattered to Jet. She pulled Mildread and Maudelin and Gideon aside and said, 'Something very strange is going on around here.'

'You've just noticed that, have you?' said Mildread.

'No, but suddenly, out of the blue, a troupe of circus performers arrive in a hot air balloon and nobody is thinking about Birdy anymore. And since when do circus performers travel in hot air balloons?'

'Since our caravans were burnt down by a mob of angry villagers,' said Lucinda Creek. 'We took the canvas from our performance tents and took to the skies. We barely escaped with our lives intact.'

She said this so matter-of-factly that the others weren't sure they'd heard her right. She had silently joined their huddle without any of them noticing.

'Where is the rest of your troupe,' asked Jet, sounding a little too accusatory for Lucinda's liking (for she still had the sound of the angry mob ringing in her ears).

'We lost them in the fog.'

'How convenient.'

'Not really. My parents were in the other balloons and all of our food supplies and circus gear. It's very inconvenient to lose them all, if you must know.'

'Is there a chance they could have perished over the sea?' asked Maudelin, hopefully.

'Every chance of it, I suppose,' said Lucinda. 'But I'd rather not think about it.'

'Oh, yes, quite right,' said Maudelin. It was hard to remember that not everybody welcomed death into the fold.

'Perhaps they were rescued by a sea creature,' suggested Mildread.

'What are the chances of that happening?' Lucinda frowned.

'Not as unlikely as you might think,' said Mildread.

'Can we please forget about sea monsters and concentrate on Birdy,' said Jet, impatiently.

'Who or what is a Birdy?' asked Lucinda.

'Birdy Black is my guardian,' said Jet, 'or at least she was before we found out she's a witch. She fell off the cliff and now there's no sign of her. All we found down there was a crow and Birdy says witches can shape-shift into any animal they choose so I'm certain that crow is Birdy in disguise.'

'And to think we were calling her Miss Crawford,' said Mildread. 'All this time we thought she was a greedy little bird pecking at our windows but it seems she's been spying on us and watching our every move.'

'And eating all our food,' added Maudelin.

'She's probably still watching us now,' said Gideon, peering nervously about.

'Yes but she won't be able to do anything about it,' said Jet. 'Not with the whole town watching.'

'Let me get this straight,' said Lucinda. 'You've only just realised that a witch who goes by the name of Birdy can actually turn into a bird? Wouldn't her name have been a dead give-away?'

'Huh,' said Jet. 'You know I never thought of it like that before.'

'Gideon's a Byrd, too,' said Maudelin helpfully.

'Yes, but I'm not an actual bird,' said Gideon, 'so it doesn't really count.'

'Oh my,' said Lucinda. 'Where on earth have I landed?'

'Smack bang in the middle of it,' said Jet, gleefully. 'Come on, I've got a feeling we'll find all the answers we need in Wildwood. And this time, Birdy can't stop us.'

Birdy (or Miss Crawford, if you prefer) might not have been able to stop them in the flesh but there is more than one way to skin a cat.

Death is all around us

Sorry, I didn't mean to conjure up such a disturbing image but you know how the Bellwethers love such vivid descriptions of the dead.

Whilst the rest of the townsfolk searched for Birdy around the cliff face, Lucinda followed Gideon and the girls down to the hedgerow and stile. When they reached the blood-plum tree, they lifted their lantern up high and turned around in confusion.

'Where are the woods?'

And well may they wonder for the fog that hung so low over the village had all but obliterated the trees so that all that was now visible of the magnificent wood was the lone plum tree, the mist hiding the branch that stretched over the hedgerow. The sky was eerily quiet. For once there were no crows watching their every move.

'At least we know Birdy isn't following us,' said Mildread.

'Never mind that,' said Jet. And she began to climb over the stile. At once she disappeared from view.

'Jet!' the others cried out, but her voice called back, 'I'm here.'

Reluctantly they followed until all of them were swallowed up by the fog. They could see nothing in front of their eyes and nothing behind them. They continued walking, calling out constantly to be sure that they all were accounted for, though none could see another in their path.

'How can we be sure we're in the wild wood?' asked Gideon.

'I'm hopelessly lost,' said Maudelin. 'Is that your hand?'

'No, not mine,' said Mildread.

In fact nobody seemed to own the hand and so Maudelin quickly let go. She didn't want to say so but it troubled her greatly that she could no longer feel a connection to Mildread. Mildread also felt the bond between them loosen and float away but since they also could no longer read each other's minds, neither one knew that the other one shared the same fear.

'Birdy Black has got the better of us again,' said Jet, 'but maybe Pete can help.'

'Who's Pete?'

'Oh, didn't I mention him? He's a boy who lives here in Wildwood, been here a long time by the looks of it. He's the one who showed me the gravesite. He helped me get away from Birdy the last time I was in here. Are you sure I haven't told you about him?'

'Are you sure that he's not just a figment of your overactive imagination,' grumbled Gideon.

'Of course he's not. Pete! Pete! Where are you?'

'If you'd stop making so much noise, you'd be able to hear me,' said a voice very close to them.

'Well that's not creepy,' said Lucinda.

'You scared us half to death,' said Gideon from the gloom.

The lantern was lifted higher until a circle of light illuminated the scruffy-looking boy.

'When you've all stopped complaining, follow me,' said Pete.

'But how? Our lantern is useless in this thick fog.'

'I've got an idea,' said Lucinda. She pulled out an enormous pair of bellows that had been strapped to her back. 'We use this to blow air into our balloons.'

'Use what?' Nobody could see a thing.

She started pumping the bellows and the fog swirled away from her, clearing a path for them to traverse.

'This way,' said Pete. He took the lead (and the bellows) and headed deeper into the thicket. The others followed in a straight line, their lantern showing the way.

Thus began the ducking and weaving and avoiding a stick in the eye.

Jet found it much easier going the second time around and the others did their best to keep up. In no time at all they were back at the river and Pete was instructing them to not look down as, wide-eyed in the water, I waited for them to walk right over the top of me.

And so everyone looked up, only to find that the crows were waiting patiently for them on the other side of the river. As they descended from the trees in a flurry of feathers and beating wings, the fog shifted out to the edge of the wood and the gravesite was fully revealed.

And there stood Birdy Black.

'Come across,' she commanded. 'The Ghost of the River Grim shall not harm you.'

'She's not the one we're afraid of,' said Gideon.

'I'm not afraid of anyone,' said Jet, head up and chin out. 'But if it's all the same with you, Birdy, I think we'll stay right where we are; safe and sound on this side of the riverbank.'

'What can you know about safety?'

'We know an evil witch when we see one.'

'Really? And what do you see?'

'Death,' whispered Mildread and Maudelin (a little too eagerly).

'How right you are. Death is all around us. Can you not feel it in your bones?'

'Yes,' whispered Mildread and Maudelin (a little less eagerly).

'Then come across and see for yourself how close to death you really are.'

Her invitation was naturally ignored but there was no denying Birdy had their undivided attention.

'Let me tell you a story, then,' she said. 'Perhaps it will allay your fears. It is a story that began a very long time ago with a broken lighthouse, a monster whale, and a shipwreck on the shore...'

'Oh good,' said Jet, 'three of my favourite things,' forgetting momentarily that Birdy was not to be trusted.

And so standing on that riverbank, not far from where I lay, the story, and the secrets, began to unfold.

Once there was a magnificent ship full of brave adventurers who sailed across the seas (began Birdy) but by the time they reached Bitterly Bay, the weather had turned wild and unpredictable. Sudden squalls lifted the sails and pushed the ship towards the rocks. A bolt of lightning lit up the sky and struck the lighthouse beacon, causing a huge crack to open up all the way down to the base and pitching the shoreline into darkness.

Oh, it was a frightful night and not one person on that ship thought they would make it out alive. As the ship began to break apart, a monster whale reared up from the waves and attempted to push them away from the rocks and safely into the shore. But it was too late.

'What do you mean it was too late?' demanded Jet. 'I never heard of a shipwreck in Bitterly Bay. When did this happen?'

'What about the wreckage lying near the jetty?' suggested Mildread. 'We see that ship, and the skeleton of a whale lying beside it, almost every day. Haven't you ever wondered how it got there?'

Jet looked at her incredulously. 'You mean it's been right under our noses all this time? Why has no one ever mentioned it before?'

'Some people don't like to be reminded of tragedies,' said Birdy.

'Well, we're not like that,' said Jet.

'I know,' smiled Birdy. 'Why don't you come across and take a look for yourself at those who perished in the wreck.'

'This could be a trick,' whispered Gideon.

And whilst the others agreed that it most certainly could be, it still did not stop them from wanting to look. I'm afraid their curiosity was too keen. And so they bravely stepped across the river stones (taking care not to look down into my deadened eyes) and gathered at the first headstone on the other side of the riverbank.

HERE LIES
CAPTAIN HORATIO PETTIFOGGER

'But that can't be,' gasped Mildread. 'Mr Pettifogger can't be a sea captain. He can't swim, his wife said so.'

'It must be his father,' said Maudelin.

'It is not his father,' said Birdy.

'What are you saying?' said Gideon, feeling the panic rise in his chest.

'She's saying Captain Pettifogger is dead,' said Maudelin.

'Which means the Mayor of Bitterly Bay is a ghost,' said Jet, with a certain degree of satisfaction.

'Does his wife know?' asked Gideon.

Birdy stepped aside to reveal the next headstone

HERE LIES
CAROLINE PETTIFOGGER
BELOVED WIFE

'Oh.'

'And to think a rotting corpse could still put on such airs and graces,' said Mildread, suitably impressed.

'Well, it explains why he put that ridiculous traffic light in the middle of main street,' said Maudelin. 'Obviously he's trying to avoid another tragedy.'

'Yes, but how does a ghost and his wife manage to run an entire town?' said Gideon.

'This is Bitterly Bay we're talking about,' said Jet. 'It makes perfect sense to me.'

'Who else died in the shipwreck?' asked Mildread, and she leant in closer to get a better view of all the other graves.

The dead cannot remain buried forever

And so there, amongst the shadows of the dead, the rest of the ship's passengers were slowly revealed.

Mrs Dimple was the ship's cook. She'd been making coffee for the Captain when the accident occurred and hadn't been able to stomach the stuff since. Of course, she didn't remember why. Like all of the passengers on that ship, she'd buried the awful truth deep in the darkest recesses of her mind.

But unpleasant things once thought dead and buried cannot remain so forever. And speaking of unpleasant things…

Mr Blatherskite was the navigator. With a little digging, he would have seen that he blamed himself for the wreck and that was why he investigated all transportation accidents. Subconsciously, he hoped that he might learn how to prevent another tragedy from occurring even though his mind refused to acknowledge the first one.

I know it seemed like he despised the children but, in reality, it was his own (buried) incompetence that made him so ill-mannered and intractable.

It was a heavy burden that he (subconsciously) carried and one that was (entirely) unnecessary. But those who (secretly) blame themselves rarely give themselves a break.

Constables Ray and Jay were petty officers, in charge of keeping everything running smoothly. Apparently the last words they spoke before being swallowed up by the sea was 'Try not to panic.'

Although they couldn't remember why, they carried that message with them and believed that, on some level, it was the key to an ordered existence.

Louisa and Cornelius Fossle…

'Not my grandparents,' cried Gideon. 'They can't be ghosts, too!'

But, of course, they very easily could.

'I think I know where this is going,' said Jet, and she led the others to the grave that she had uncovered the last time she was there. 'I thought that Birdy was trying to kill me because of this…'

She pointed to a headstone.

HERE LIES
JET
A BRAVE &
FEARLESS EXPLORER

'It's all coming back to me now. I remember being on that ship, climbing over the handrails and hiding down in the bowels of the boiler room.'

'What are you saying?' gasped Gideon. 'Are you saying that you're... a ghost?'

'Of course she is,' said Birdy. 'She watched in horror as the ship broke up on the rocks and she watched in disbelief as her body washed up along the shores of Bitterly Bay. I tried to help her cross over into the afterlife but she didn't want to go. She didn't want to be dead.'

'I didn't,' said Jet. 'But I am, aren't I? I really am.'

'I knew there was a reason why we liked you so much,' said Maudelin.

'So Birdy wasn't trying to kill you, she was trying to help you remember. She's not an evil witch, after all,' said Lucinda.

'But what about the story of Birdy finding Jet on her doorstep when she was just a baby?' asked Gideon.

'I did find Jet on my doorstep,' said Birdy, 'or at least her spirit. She was frightened and confused. She had been a stowaway on the ship, in search of adventure, and had no family to help her transition over to the other side, from the world of the living to the realm of the dead. And so I stepped in to help. But Jet found it hard to accept her death. Children, as a general rule, find it much harder than adults. Perhaps it's because they were not given the chance to live a full and robust life. And so things got a little murky. It was easier to believe that I had found Jet on my doorstep when she was just a baby.'

'But why did you dress up as an old lady?' asked Jet.

'If you were a baby when I supposedly found you, then I should have aged over the ensuing years. You would say to me, "Why do you not age? You look the same as the day you found me but I was just a baby then and now I am much older." and I would reply that you were not a baby when I found you and that you would never get any older because you were dead and, oh, the wailing and screeching that you would do. It was enough to wake the dead. Sorry, no pun intended.'

'So you decided it would just be easier to perpetuate the lie?' suggested Lucinda.

Perhaps the circus made it easier for her to accept a world of make-believe.

'Time does not move on when you are dead,' explained Birdy, 'but since Jet refused to believe she was dead, I was forced to appear older to avoid any further confusion, hence my elderly disguise. Thank goodness that is all over now.'

She ran her fingers through her thick, black hair, all traces of the talcum powder gone.

'Does that mean Jet has to leave us?' asked Maudelin. 'I don't want her to go.'

'Me neither,' said Mildread.

Gideon nodded in agreement but Lucinda was staring at the sky and thinking of her circus troupe.

'We didn't make it through that storm, did we?'

Birdy took her hand and squeezed it. 'You were very brave, my dear, but the cold took you all in the end.'

'Do the others know?'

'Ringo realised the truth when he saw Mademoiselle. He was in Paris when she died.'

'What? Mademoiselle is dead, too?' Mildread looked shocked.

'But didn't our mother send her to watch over us?' said Maudelin. 'Is our mother dead, too?'

'No, Elizabeth is not dead,' said Birdy. 'And that is why she cannot be reunited with her family just yet. Your mother and your Aunt Emily are not dead but...'

Slowly the fog lifted...

And there they were, amongst the rest of the passengers that had died in the shipwreck.

HERE LIES
BYRON BELLWETHER
BELOVED HUSBAND AND FATHER

HERE LIES
MILDREAD & MAUDELIN
BELLWETHER
INSEPERABLE IN LIFE
TOGETHER IN DEATH

HERE LIES
OLGA
(Surname Unknown)
FAITHFUL GOVERNESS & COOK

Let the dead have death

Finding out you are dead can be an awful shock to the system. I remember the moment when I realised I was a ghost. It's bad enough my bones are rotting away in a watery grave but to have all manner of man and beast clamber over the top of me without a word of apology can sometimes test me to my limit. You haven't died until you've had a leech suck out your eyeball or a river rat gnaw at your earlobe. It's a wonder I have any chance of resting in peace.

I can't say it wasn't an enormous shock to Mildread and Maudelin to find out they were dead, too, but they handled it much better than most. Considering how deathly pale and morose they were, I'm a little surprised they didn't twig sooner. But they perked right up (or whatever the gloomy equivalent is) and accepted the situation without complaint.

'It really does explain a lot,' Mildread had to admit.

'And I don't feel any different,' added Maudelin.

'But if we're all ghosts, then what is Aunt Prunella?'

'She is a ghost, too,' explained Birdy. 'She died at home in her rocking chair. But you knew that already. So when you could suddenly see her in the flesh, so to speak, you had to find a way to make sense of it. You decided that you could see a ghost, that's all. It never occurred to any of you that you might be one, too.

'How come I couldn't see her?' asked Gideon.

'You, and many others in Bitterly Bay, didn't want to accept that the dead can roam about the place but now I think you might.'

She pointed to another headstone.

HERE LIES

GIDEON BYRD

BELOVED SON & GRANDSON

'I remember now,' said Gideon.

I know what you're thinking; how is it possible that someone cannot know they are dead, but believe me when I tell you that a lot of people have great difficulty in accepting this.

It seems to be the pattern that once the barrier of denial has been removed, the memories flood back and the truth can finally be revealed.

'I was travelling with my grandparents,' said Gideon. 'But what about my mother, I don't remember her being on the trip?'

'Ah, that is complicated,' said Birdy.

But then everything about Dottie Byrd was complicated.

Dottie was not on the ship but she lost her senses completely when she found out her son and parents had died. She wanted to be with them so badly that I'm afraid she took her own life. When she woke to find them with her, she thought it had all been a bad dream, especially since life in Bitterly Bay seemed to have continued happily on, with no one mentioning the sticky truth.

Don't get me wrong, Birdy did try to tell them, but no one was ready to believe her. Sometimes it can take a while for a dead person to process such a life-altering event.

Only Mademoiselle seemed aware that everyone was dead. It was the jet beads that she'd sewn into the lining of her petticoat that was Dottie's undoing.

Some believe that if you stitch jet (worn in mourning) into the clothing of the dead, you can ease their transition over to the other side and so Dottie, in her usual muddled way, figured that if she stole the beads and hid them then somehow death could be held at bay.

Dottie wasn't ready to mourn anyone just yet but the truth of what had happened kept intruding into her mind until it drove her so batty that she feared she was losing her marbles.

And that's when she decided to run over the Bellwether twins in the delivery van in the middle of Main Street.

She wanted to know just how far this conspiracy went. She had seen Gideon talking to Mildread and Maudelin outside the butcher shop. So it stood to reason that if Gideon could see them and speak to them, too, then that must mean that whatever they were, alive or dead, they were all in it together. She couldn't possibly run over her son with the van. What if she was wrong and he was alive after all? That would surely kill him and then she'd be back where she started from; mourning his death and wishing herself dead, too, and so she thought it best to aim her deadly vehicle at 'those morbid twins' instead.

She truly believed that they would be less likely to kick up a fuss if she killed them, on account of how much they seemed to adore being around death.

Curse their nimble feet, leaping out of harm's way just in the nick of time. At least she'd managed to run over the offal stuffed in their shopping bag. It smelt so rotten that she had no trouble believing *that* was dead. Mind you, she now questioned whether everything dead ought to smell as bad. Was nobody dead if they didn't smell as rotten as that package? Could she have been wrong all along?

She couldn't help it. She had to be sure one way or the other. She watched Mademoiselle sell books and her father, Cornelius Fossle, sell a fishing rod to Jet, then watched Jet and her mother, Louisa Fossle, talking to the twins out the front of the teashop, and she watched Mrs Dimple talking to them inside it, and so clearly whatever the truth was, it involved everyone. Was no one spared? She was getting rather desperate.

It was only a teeny, tiny explosion, she reasoned, and she hadn't really meant for the entire ceiling to collapse but when every single person emerged unscathed from Mrs Dimple's teashop, then she knew the truth. Everybody was dead, but only *she* seemed to know it.

'I've lost my marbles,' she would tell anyone who would listen but what if she was referring to actual marbles? I think she might have been talking about those beads. And I think I know where they are. Remember the bag of blackened eyeballs in the window of the Shipwreck Shop? I said they could have been mouldy marbles but what if they were the jet beads, hiding in plain sight all along?

Once Birdy had explained everything, Jet asked the obvious. 'Why didn't she just tell us that we'd all died in a shipwreck?'

'Would you have believed her?'

'Well, no. She's nuts.'

'Exactly.'

'But what about Uncle Barnaby's boat?' said Maudelin. 'Why did she have to blow that up? It was a beautiful old boat and deserved better than a watery grave.'

'Did my mother really blow that up, too?' asked Gideon, weakly.

'No,' said Birdy, 'there was no bomb on Barnaby's boat. Nobody tampered with the engine or caused the boat to sink. No investigation is needed to get to the bottom of things. It is simply the rule that all of the dead must follow...'

In fact, when you get right down to it, it is the only rule (had the Bellwethers not insisted on adding all those others) that must be strictly adhered to...

The dead can never return to the realm of the living.

They can never leave Bitterly Bay.

They can never cross the sea.

There is nothing out there for them but the unending ocean of nothingness.

Everything has a beginning and an end

It is the job of a few of the living, the ones we know as witches, to keep the living from the dead and the dead away from the living. They are the only ones imbued with the power to straddle both realms – one foot in the land of the living and one foot in the world of the dead – and they consider it an enormous privilege to be able to see both worlds at once. Birdy Black feels fortunate to live in her cottage between the lighthouse and the Bellwethers and betwixt the living and the dead.

When she walks into town, she can see the living going about their business whilst the dead, seen only by her, weave in amongst their legs and lean over the countertops in front of their unseeing eyes.

When the ancient old tea urn in the teashop hisses and splutters of its own accord, she is the only one who can see Mrs Dimple fiddling with the levers and pouring a restorative brew for one of her unseen customers.

When people trip up upon entering The Abandoned Book Shop, she is the only one who can see Mademoiselle sitting on the old chair in the doorway.

When the pedestrians feel the wind pushing them down the footpath, only Birdy can see Mrs Fossle, bustling them along.

And when Uncle Barnaby's boat chugs its way out of the bay, the only one who can see it is Birdy. But sometimes, if the sea breeze is particularly strong and the fog is lifted away, you just might be able to see Emily Bellwether standing on the clifftop, searching vainly for her true love's return.

'You cannot ever leave this ghost town,' Birdy explained. 'Every time Barnaby's boat reaches the limits of the otherworld, you are turned back, one way or another.'

'By capsizing the boat, if necessary?' asked Mildread.

'That's right.'

'But if Mademoiselle knew we were all dead, then why did she try to keep us from drowning?'

'She wasn't trying to stop a tragedy; she was trying to stop you from learning the truth too harshly. We have both discussed this at length and she was of the firm opinion, as was I, that you all needed to be led gently to the truth. She feared the shock of discovering it too quickly might cause irreparable damage. She had seen what it had done to Dottie and she did not want to see it do the same to you. And so first she ran down to the dock to try to stop you from leaving, and then she rushed to the police to tell them all about a tragedy at sea. She was, of course, referring to the night of the shipwreck but she realised at once that no one wanted to believe her and so she quickly let the matter drop.'

'So we weren't really in danger of drowning?'

'No. But it would have caused great consternation had you sunk to the bottom of the bay, only to return shortly thereafter as right as rain.'

'And what about the sea creature that saved me?' asked Mildread.

'The ghost of that poor whale still haunts these shores, forever trying to save you from the sea. You ought to visit him one day and issue a thank you. I'm sure it would be greatly appreciated. He's really rather sweet. I think his name is Herman.'

'But why did you teach me to swim if you knew I couldn't drown?' asked Jet.

'So that you would not realise it, of course.'

'And the clifftop crumbling into the sea?' asked Gideon. 'Who was responsible for that?'

'The most powerful force of all – Mother Nature,' explained Birdy. 'Just ask Uncle Barnaby how violent she can get.'

'Wait a minute,' said Maudelin, 'is Uncle Barnaby even dead? I don't remember him being on that shipwreck.'

'He was not on the ship but he did die at sea, just the way he would have wanted it.'

'But how did he get here?' asked Mildread.

'His faithful boat, drifting across the sea, finally brought him home.'

'So when he turned up dead, just like the rest of us, we were the only ones who could see him?'

'That's right. Emily still stands on the clifftop, waiting to catch a glimpse of his boat and sometimes you can see her, so strong is her desire to connect with him.'

Usually the dead can't see the living and the living can't see the dead but sometimes things can bleed through if the vibrations are strong enough. Love is a particularly strong emotion that frequently bridges the gap.

'Poor Aunt Emily,' said Maudelin, 'waiting all this time for news of Uncle Barnaby's fate.'

'She spends a great deal of time on that clifftop,' Birdy explained. 'I have tried to tell her what happened but she refuses to listen. One day they shall be reunited, when the time comes for her to cross over to the other side.'

'Well how about that,' said Jet, shaking her head. 'All this time we were trying to figure out what horrible fate had befallen Aunt Emily and it turns out she was perfectly safe all along. Alive and kicking.'

'And we were the ones who were dead,' grinned Gideon.

He didn't seem half as bothered as he thought he would at the idea of being dead. He'd spent most of his life afraid that something awful would happen and now that it had, he realised it wasn't the worst thing in the world. In fact, being dead was really rather liberating.

He had nothing left to fear. It felt like a huge weight had suddenly lifted off him. Not to mention, the relief he felt at knowing that his mother hadn't actually killed anyone. And what a surprise to learn that she wasn't batty after all!

He was almost giddy with relief.

He turned to Maudelin and said, 'By the way, I didn't thank you for coming to my rescue in the lighthouse.'

Maudelin leant in close and kissed three of the freckles on Gideon's cheek. 'Now we're even,' she said.

Gideon blushed the colour of his freckles.

Yes, being dead didn't feel bad at all.

Mildread gave a little smile. Perhaps this blossoming friendship wasn't the worst that could happen. Possibly it no longer bothered her because she was just happy to *not* be alive. I told you death brought out the best in them. But one thing still bothered her.

'Why did you kidnap Gideon and truss him up like a turkey?' she asked Birdy.

'I had to think of something to stop you all from blundering upon the truth. I simply wanted to divert your attention from the graveyard in the woods and let the others calm down a little. And it worked, didn't it? I feared that if you were suddenly confronted all at once it might cause untold panic and distress but, I must say, you're taking this much better than I expected.'

'And what about our mother?' asked Maudelin. 'You haven't told us what happened to her.'

Birdy's eyes instantly lit up for Elizabeth Bellwether was quite a formidable woman and I do not doubt that many books will be written about her one day. I feel privileged to include her in this one.

Elizabeth, you see, was an adventuress. She travelled the globe and boldly ventured where few would dare to tread. I think Jet would like her immensely, were they ever to meet and although I have made it perfectly clear that only witches can communicate with the dead, I must admit that Elizabeth, though not a witch, might very well be the exception to this seemingly unbreakable rule.

She was the only one, to my knowledge, to ever have come close to lifting the veil between the living and the dead. When Mademoiselle was on her (rather elaborate) deathbed, Elizabeth insisted that she would find a way to reach her dearly departed loved ones. She wore that jet necklace, day in, day out, ever since the day she had learned of the shipwreck. She wore it in the bathtub, she wore it on excavations and during elaborate banquets with The Queen. She wore it as she clambered through the fairy caves in Görome and ballooning over the Eiffel Tower. When she finally sewed it into Mademoiselle's death gown, it was so infused with her energy that it couldn't help but carry a piece of her along with it.

Elizabeth was not dead – far, far, from it – but her presence was so keenly felt in the ghost town of Bitterly Bay, that, I don't know how, but every time she sent a trinket home to the Bellwether estate, it was received by the dead (along with the living).

Do you remember me telling you that heavy objects were left at the foot of the stair, where they somehow found their way into the attic? Well, it was the living relatives who lugged it up those stairs and into the attic where Prunella lovingly dusted it and stored it for safe keeping.

I know I am not wrong in saying that Elizabeth had the power to lift the spirits of every family member in the Bellwether house, be they living or dead, and that, my friend, is an incredible ability to possess.

Like I said, she was a truly amazing person.

And there's no need to get too morbid for life does carry on to a certain extent, even after death. Ghostly shopkeepers open their ghostly shops; ghostly children climb their ghostly trees and swing their ghostly legs into the ghostly gloom. There's quite a bit of gloom, by the way. Bright light and sunshine rarely exist in the afterlife. It's more of a muted grey (far more flattering). And then there's the fog.

Listen very carefully for this is quite important.

The fog is what protects the hereafter from the great abyss of nothingness. It encircles the island, the woods, and the bay, and the dead cannot cross it. They can never go beyond the mist and it is the witch's duty to keep them safely within it.

When someone dies and finds themselves lost in Bitterly Bay, it is Birdy's duty to welcome them warmly and show them that life, in another form, does indeed go on.

Usually it is a fairly painless process but the dead of Bitterly Bay have proven to be difficult souls to salvage. Stubborn, I think Birdy would say. Perhaps there is something in the water?

Well, besides me, of course.

'I tried for a very long time to bring you all here to witness your own graves,' explained Birdy, 'but the harder I tried, the less inclined you were to acquiesce. So I tried a little reverse psychology. I told you *not* to come in here and naturally you did the opposite. It took quite some time but I was prepared to wait. After all, time is what you have in abundance when you are dead.'

Birdy turned to Pete Moss and said, 'Speaking of time, don't you think the time has come for you to leave the woods? I have been trying to find you for so long. You're quite the slippery one.'

Pete looked down at a tiny grave (suitable for a very skinny boy) and said, 'Is that my body buried there?' And as he looked down at his grave, he, too, remembered. 'Oh! I was a cabin boy. I found Jet as a stowaway and promised to keep her safe.'

Jet looked disappointed but was quick to explain that it had nothing to do with Pete.

'I thought he might have been the body that we found buried beneath the blackberry bush,' she confessed. 'I figured he was the only one of us unaccounted for.'

'Ah, yes, the body beneath the blackberry bush,' smiled Birdy.

Now what if I were to tell you, dear reader, that the corpse's clawed hand did indeed hold a book; this very book, in fact. That's right. This book contains all of the rules that the dead need to know in order for them to cross over to the other side. It is a manual, if you will, a guide that you have hopefully found helpful.

Have you realised the truth about the body beneath the blackberry bush?

It's you.

I don't know how you ended up buried beneath the blackberry bush (although just between you and me, I suspect foul play in both our cases), but none of that matters anymore. I am sure that eventually when you're ready to face it, you will remember. Until then, there's nothing you can do about it, so might I recommend you forget about your troubles and embrace all the wondrous possibilities that death has opened up for you.

If you want to know the truth of it, I'm beginning to think that I, too, have spent far too long rotting in my grave. I think it's time we both got a new perspective, don't you? As Proust would say, the real voyage of discovery consists not in seeking new landscapes but in having new eyes (and we could both do with a new pair of those!).

Personally, I'm looking forward to getting into some dry clothes. And I think perhaps a new name. Being called The Ghost of the River Grim can be a little depressing at times and suddenly I'm feeling rather optimistic. I don't remember what I once was called (forgive me, but it has been a long time), but I rather like the name Ophelia.

And, likewise, there is nothing holding you back now, my friend. So close this book and open your mind, and welcome to Bitterly Bay.

Or, as the Bellwethers would say…

Everything has a beginning.
And an end.
Even me.
Even you.
And even this story, too.

Oh, and look on the bright side; the circus has come to town.

THE END

Life is for the living
Let the dead have death

Kerry Mitchell

Also Available

From One Extreme to the Other
{A book of poetry}

The Witch's Tale
{A book of rhyming fairy tales}

Coming Soon

Theodora van Runkle
{Be careful what you wish for}